Anna Harriet Drury

Deep Waters

Vol. III

Anna Harriet Drury

Deep Waters
Vol. III

ISBN/EAN: 9783337066871

Printed in Europe, USA, Canada, Australia, Japan

Cover: Foto ©Andreas Hilbeck / pixelio.de

More available books at **www.hansebooks.com**

DEEP WATERS

A Novel.

BY

ANNA H. DRURY,

AUTHOR OF "MISREPRESENTATION," "FRIENDS AND FORTUNE," &c.

IN THREE VOLUMES.

VOL. III.

LONDON:

CHAPMAN AND HALL, 193, PICCADILLY.

1863.

CONTENTS OF VOL. III.

DEEP WATERS.

CHAPTER I.

THE WIFE'S SECRET.

THE peril that surrounded them, even at such a moment, constrained them to exercise self-control, and that first passionate embrace was given almost in silence—only broken by the low rapid whispers of endearment, tenderness, and joy, that could reach no human ear but that to which they were breathed. Clinging round his neck with both hands, as if she could not otherwise realise he was there, with

her head resting on his bosom, all she had
suffered seemed nothing to Eleanor now : she
felt, she understood nothing, but that he was
returned—that she had regained him—and
that he loved her. The past was as if it had
never been—he was here, and he was her own,
and whatever he came to tell her, whatever
might lie in the unrevealed future, she was
strong enough to brave, so long as they braved
it together. "My love! my own! come back
to me at last!" she repeated several times, as
she raised her head from his bosom to look into
his face, and convince herself it was not a
cruel dream. " You will not leave me again
—you are come to tell me so !"

" I am come to tell you a great deal, my
Eleanor, that cannot be said in a moment, or
here. Come a few steps farther; there is a
seat this way." He hurried her on as he
spoke, till they reached a wooden summer-
house, where Arthur was in the habit of being
wheeled on warm afternoons. Here Atter-

bury seated his wife, and then without relinquishing his clasp, knelt on the ground at her feet.

" Forgive me, Eleanor—say you forgive me !"

" My own, my dearest — can you doubt me ?" she returned ; " you said you would trust me, and I tried to deserve your trust. You thought you were doing for the best, I know, and your own sufferings must have been greater than mine. You are come back, and I ask nothing more, only that you do not leave me again."

He made no reply; but his head rested against her, while his arms encircled her as he knelt. Her hand caressed his cheek, and found it wet with his tears.

" Let them be," he said, in broken accents; " they do me good. I have been leading the life of a dog so long, this comfort makes a woman of me. My guardian angel—but for the thought of you, I should never have lived through these two years. How I have done so, seems a miracle. Men died all round me—honest men, who had names they need not hide—whose honour no one doubted—I, who would have thanked death for taking me, always escaped. Either I was not worth taking, or your prayers were too strong."

"They were all I had left to give you," was her whispered reply.

"I know it; you gave up everything for my honour. I hoped to save you from robbery by my flight; I did not know you would rob yourself—but I might have guessed it. Oh, Eleanor, how had you ever deserved so cruel a fate?"

"I have you once more; never mind the past. God has been very merciful to us. At one time I thought I should never see you again."

"You were very ill, then?"

"Very ill, dearest." She bowed her head over his as she said this, for the sorrow of that illness was more than she could speak of calmly, and for a little while both were silent. But there was too much for each to ask and learn, for many of these precious minutes to be lost. Above all, she wanted to understand his present condition—why he had come back, and how he had discovered her retreat.

"My condition," he said, "is that of an outlaw; every man's hand is against me, and any one who can make me his prisoner, may claim the reward—that I knew when I came. I had resolved, when I left you, not to burden you further—not to give you any opportunity of sending me money, or of following me into exile. I clung to the hope that you would thus be spared a great deal of misery, that your friends would come round you, and take you perhaps abroad, where, though I knew you could not be happy, you, at least, would live in comfort. Meanwhile, I would work hard from morning till night, till I could offer you a respectable home in America, where my name would no longer be your disgrace. This was the dream that kept me from the lowest depth of degradation and despair, for it saved me from my worst temptation, *drink*."

"Thank God! And you have succeeded?"

"How could I hope to succeed? I did hope, at first, but I found, before very long, that I was watched—that some hostile influence worked against me wherever I went, and if I had a chance of getting on for a month or two, I lost it again, on my name and story becoming public. In short, Martock's agents were on my trail, and followed me everywhere."

"I feared it. Go on—you shall know why afterwards. Did you hear from him?"

"No; but it must have been through his people that a paragraph went round the American papers, all about my affairs, and stating that you were last heard of, in indigent circumstances, and weak health, serving in a menial capacity, and under a feigned name. Let who might, however, have spread the story, it decided my plans. I only waited till I had raised money enough for a steerage passage home. I had been lodging with some honest Germans, to whom I had shown some little kindness, and the poor man, who was a photographer, was dying when I left, so I bought his apparatus, and got myself up as like him as I could. I believe no one would ever have known me. You did not, at any rate."

"No, indeed. But how did you find me out?"

"I went to Shannon's office, but he was out of town on some suit of his own, and at first, no one would give me any clue to your whereabout. But at last, the old clerk, to whom I confided that I was the bearer of private intelligence to you from your husband, told me you had been living, he knew, with a Mrs. Cummings, whose address he gave. I went down there—part of the way on foot, taking portraits occasionally to pay my way—and having

inquired cautiously for you in the place, learned
you were now living here. I was too well
known in these parts to risk discovery. I did
not know how far you might have trusted
these new friends, and they were the last I
could meet undisguised. But a description
that I read at an inn of a birthday fête at
Lawleigh, suggested to me, knowing the
family weakness about the old place, to try
whether a little flattery on that head would
not obtain me the opportunity of privately
communicating with you. I would not have
done so, but I durst not do otherwise."

"Then you have been here before? You
know the Claverings?"

"I wish I could say I did not. Eleanor—
is she—is Anne good to you?"

"She has been kindness itself—they all
have. She suffers from depression at times,
but she is so good and generous, I can bear all
that."

"Has she any idea who you are?"

" No—how should she? But I do not understand—she knows *you*, then?"

" To her sorrow."

" Frederick—you frighten me! I am easily
frightened now. Oh, tell me the truth at
once, for I hardly dare to think——"

" I will. You shall know all you have
to pardon. That anonymous present of
yours——"

" The bracelet? I brought it here to give
you—all I have left—in case you wanted
money. What of it?"

" Cannot you guess who sent it to you?"

She was dumb; he could hardly hear her
breathe. He tasted in that moment the fruit
of what he had sown.

" Eleanor, before I knew you, I knew and
loved Anne Clavering; but I wronged her less
than I have wronged you, for desertion was a
lighter injury than marriage. It is from you
who have had most to bear, that I have most
hope of forgiveness. Do not turn from me—

hear me one moment! Thank God, the truth
is spoken, and you know the worst, and I have
nothing more to tell. I could not keep my
vow to her, for I was plunged in debt, and my
father would not help me unless I married a
woman of fortune. Yes, you may well shudder,
and shrink from me; the time for pitying me
is not yet come: you will, by-and-bye, when
you think what it must be to have to own this.
I saw you—I won your love—and what was
to have been my punishment, became my sal-
vation—who could be with you, and not love
you, and love goodness for your sake? Miserable as I was, and as you saw me, it was as
much from self-reproach at having brought
wretchedness on such an angel, as all the rest
of my burdens put together. That day at
Twalmley, when I rested my head on your
knees, oh, what would I have given to have
undone the past, to have been able to make
you happy, to have had a conscience at rest,
even if I had bought it with a lifetime of

pain! I was never so near the utter despair
that drives men to suicide, as that night when
I left you; and only the thought of your love
and mercy saved me from that crowning sin.
You know now the wretch you married—can
you love and pardon him still?"

If she could, she **had** not yet the power of
expressing it. Her brain **was** dizzy with the
rush of recollections, the fearfully vivid light
thrown on past events that had seemed so unintelligible before.

"Miss Clavering—is it possible? Miss Clavering! And she knows now who I am—she
recognised the bracelet—she has been different
to me ever since—no wonder! And after all
her sweet kindness, to be the one whom she
could least bear to see! Oh, Frederick!"
burying her face on his shoulder, "tell me
this, at least, if you would keep my heart
from breaking—which of us is dearest to you
now?"

"I have deserved the question," said he,

mournfully, "and the answer is worth very little. But, Eleanor, if you can believe a dishonoured man, whose last wealth you are—I have only one object now to make life endurable, and that is to be more worthy of *you*. I have told you the truth at all hazards—but could I have done it, if I had not wished my whole heart to be devoted and open to you, henceforth? Listen," as he sat down on the bench beside her, and supported her on his breast, "listen, my own dear wife. You do not know what you have done for me; you have given me a motive for repentance and change of life that no one ever did. I saw what my past life had been, when I saw what you were; and if I am allowed to live, and to escape, all I ask now is to redeem it by the hardest work—anywhere, of any kind—to have a conscience at peace, and hope for pardon from Heaven. But you must help me, for if I have lost your love, I dare not hope. Look, Eleanor —my hands are hard with labour—of such rough kinds, too, as you have never seen—but card, or dice-box, or betting-book, or borrowed money, or a crust that was not paid for, I have not touched since I left England, and never will—so help me God, who gave me this last hold on Himself—the prayers of a wife like you!"

"I knew He would hear them—I knew it," she said, "and you shall never have cause to repent your openness with me—never. All is well lost, if you——" A long fit of coughing, which she vainly tried to smother, interrupted the sentence, and alarmed Atterbury not a little. He drew her cloak round her, and began reproaching himself for exposing her to the night air. As soon as she could speak again, she was beginning to assure him of her recovered strength, and large capacity for work and exertion, when he suddenly started up, and put his hand on her mouth. She rose too, and clinging to his arm, listened as intently as he did. Steps were distinctly audible on the other side of the hedge, and as they stood perfectly still, they became aware of a figure creeping along, stopping every now and then to watch and listen, and then creeping on again under the deep shadow. Presently, there was a whistle, and then a pause, and then the figure crept on till it was quite out of sight and hearing.

" What can that mean?" muttered Atterbury.

Eleanor recollected Adam's story, and hastily repeated it. Her husband shook his head, and seemed perplexed and dismayed.

" You must go in, love," he whispered, " go in this moment, and leave me to slip out as I came. To-morrow I will contrive another meeting, and then we will arrange——Hush!"

Footsteps were coming now from the direction of the house, and it was evident they were making for their retreat. They drew farther into the shadow, and Atterbury hastily resumed his disguise. Presently, a tall figure, with a sack on his shoulder, came into the shrubbery, looked over the hedge, whistled cautiously, and after listening for a reply, moved towards the summer-house.

"Pst! Are you there, mate?"

No answer being given, he hesitated a moment, and then opened a dark-lantern, and turned the light full on the interior of the little building as he advanced. The start he gave at the unexpected sight it revealed, made the sack slip from his shoulder, and the metallic jingle of plate was no more to be mistaken, than the sunburnt face of Mr. Clavering's confidential servant.

He saw in a moment that he was detected, and his whole manner became transformed. His eyes glittered with rage and hate, and his white teeth shone in the moonlight, as he stole his hand into his pocket for his large clasp-knife.

"So this is your fidelity to your master, is it?" said Atterbury, sternly. "Your accomplice is gone on, I can tell you ; and if you do not carry back all those valuables you are stealing to the place you took them from, I shall rouse the house, and give you into custody."

" You can speak English now, can you ?" muttered the man, with an oath ; " if I didn't feel sure there was some game going on, when I saw you! And Mrs. Mornay out here at this time of night to meet you—I doubt her wishing you to rouse the house, and I doubt your doing it, and if you are wise, you will mind your own affairs. Keep my secret, and I'll keep yours."

" You think you will bully me, you rascal ?" said Atterbury, making a stride forwards. " Out of the way this moment—and you, Eleanor, run to the house."

Adam set down the lantern, and planted himself in the doorway, in a menacing attitude. "Think twice about it, both of you. There never was a German sausage-eater yet that could frighten me."

" Out of the way !" said Atterbury, beating down his guard with one hand, and seizing his collar with the other. In the struggle that ensued, the wig and beard, hastily fastened on, became loosened, and fell to the ground. Adam staggered before the unexpected apparition, and his eyes flashed with exulting revenge. ·"It's *you*, is it? Then you shall never master me alive !" He flung Atterbury back, and unclasped his large knife. Eleanor saw it raised—the terror that had paralysed her senses gave way before that more deadly fear; she flung herself between them with a stifled shriek, and fell insensible on the ground.

When she recovered, she was lying on the floor in Anne's little room at Lawleigh, and Atterbury was supporting her on one knee. His whispers of endearment and relief as he saw her consciousness returning, fell so sweetly on her ear, she felt at first as if in a dream, from which she feared to wake; but as recollection returned, alarm quickened her energies;

she half raised herself on her elbow, and looked wildly round. The lantern stood on the table, and by its light she could see that Atterbury was deadly pale, and hardly able to sustain himself.

" What has happened? How did I come here?"

" Hush, love—ask no questions—are you better now?"

" Quite well," she returned, shivering, "only giddy, I think. Dearest, you look very ill—are you hurt?"

" That fellow slashed my arm, that is all. When you can find me something to tie it up, I shall be all right."

He was wounded; all her faintness was forgotten. She staggered to her feet, and holding by the table, tried desperately to steady her nerves.

" What had I better do? Shall I call for help?"

" Not for your life, or I am lost. Get me a basin of water if you can, and some strips for bandages, and I will show you what to do next."

She could only find Bruno's basin, which was placed full of fresh water in the passage every night. Bruno himself had disappeared; Adam having taken the precaution of locking him up. There were plenty of table-napkins in Anne's room. She cut one into strips, hoping she was committing no great breach of trust and honesty, and, sick and giddy as she still was, by strenuous efforts commanded herself sufficiently to obey all her husband's directions. His coat-sleeve was so soaked with blood, it was not easy to get it off; the gash to her eyes looked ghastly, but he assured her it was only a flesh wound, and of no consequence; and showed her how to wash and bind it up, which she did quietly and firmly; asking no questions till all was done, and she had slung his arm in his neckcloth. Then she ventured to breathe the question she had been dreading to ask, " Where is that wretched man ?"

He groaned as he replied, " I did not want to hurt him—it was his own doing—when he drew his knife, I caught hold of a stick, and after he had missed his blow, by my catching the blade on my left arm, I took care not to miss mine. He went down like a log, and I had no time to see how much he was hurt, for I had to carry you home. Here is something that fell from his pocket. You had better take care of it, if it is part of his plunder."

" It is Mr. Clavering's pocket-book, that he saw me lock up. Oh, Frederick, all this is so terrible, and you are so much hurt—let me call down Mr. Clavering, and tell him everything, and trust to his generosity."

" In this house — appear like *this* before them, and beg their compassion ? Eleanor, I would rather die."

" My dearest, you will die if you attempt to escape now, so ill and faint as you are. Oh, what was that ? Did you not hear ?"

He did hear, and the sound brought the large drops to his brow. He sprang to the lantern, and closed the slide, and both stood listening to the too audible sound of feet and voices in the garden, steadily approaching the house.

"They have found that fellow, and are bringing ' him here," whispered Atterbury, "and they will find me here, and he knows me."

Both knew what must be the result of the discovery at that moment. They clung to each other in momentary despair.

"He will denounce me directly, and I cannot face it yet, or *here*. I have my revolver—it shall be at their own risk if they try to take me!"

"Oh no, no—for the love of Heaven—for my sake!" she pleaded, clasping him as if her hold could save him from utter ruin. "Think of your promises, your vows of repentance, of God's mercy to us! Do not resist—better suffer wrong than do it—better anything than shed blood !"

The footsteps came up to the door; a hand tried the lock, but finding it secured, there was a murmur of voices in consultation, and then they were heard to move steadily on.

" They are gone to the other door," she whispered; " could you escape now by this?"

" Too late—I shall be seen, and they would run me down in a minute. Eleanor, Eleanor," —strong man as he was, he was positively trembling with his intense fear,—" can you do nothing for me?   Is there nowhere that you can hide me for an hour, or will you see me dragged away like a dog before your face ?"

Rupert Clavering had slept, after his long walk, unusually sound, and was dreaming, very probably, of old Australian scenes, long past away, when he gradually became aware of voices shouting under his window, and of the door-bell ringing with that peculiar effect which bells have when rung in the dead of night. He roused himself with a start, and, opening his window, asked who was there.

" Policeman, sir !" returned a voice that he knew well. " We have found your servant half-murdered; there has been an attempt to rob your house. We have brought him here, but we can't get in."

" I'll be with you directly."

Mr. Clavering did not waste a moment in ejaculations or inquiries; he struck a light— glanced at his watch, and saw it was just three o'clock; dressed himself with the alertness of youth, and went very quietly to rouse Nurse Moyle. She was just awake, and listening; and having made her promise to be down directly, without disturbing the ladies, Rupert hurried to open the door.

Adam looked a pitiable object, supported in the arms of the policeman and a shepherd of Mr. Maberley's; a handkerchief had been tied on his head, but the stains showed the force of the blow he had received, and his hands and dress bore testimony to his having been engaged in deadly strife.

" Poor fellow !" said his master, when they had laid him on the table, and he could take his hand, " poor fellow ! how came this about ? Why did you not call for help?"

" He says he did, sir, but no one heard him. He tells us he heard people about, so he went out to see, and they set on him—that was it, wasn't it ?" said the policeman.

" Yes," said Adam, faintly.

" Well, well, you are a brave fellow, and you shall be rewarded. But we must see to your hurt. Here comes nurse, she will be a better surgeon than I am. I say, nurse, here is a bad business. Some burglars were prowling about the place, and Adam went out after them, and they have half killed him among them. Quick, light us some candles, and then come and see what you can do."

Shocked and dismayed as Nurse Moyle was,

she refrained from expressing her feelings till she had done her utmost for the patient; but when Adam's wound had been dressed and he had swallowed some wine-and-water, the policeman began to put further questions. The answers came slowly and reluctantly; but the pain the man was suffering seemed to account for that; he stated that he had been disturbed by a noise in the garden—that he had come down to see who was there—that he had found the door in Miss Clavering's sitting-room ajar —that he had gone round the premises without seeing any one, till he got to the summer-house in the shrubbery, and there he found two people, a man and a woman; the man carrying a sack of plate which he let fall on seeing him. That he had a scuffle with the man, and wounded him with his knife; but received a blow in return, which stunned him for the time, until just before the shepherd and policeman came up.

A man and a woman? Could he swear to

them? Yes, he thought he could—to the man, he was sure—as to the woman——

He stopped short with a convulsive start, as a face appeared at the door, unexpected by all present—the pale, almost haggard face of Eleanor Atterbury.

"Mrs. Mornay! What made you get up? I hoped you would not hear," said Uncle Rupert. "I am so sorry you were disturbed."

"Was you awake, ma'am?" asked Nurse Moyle, quickly. "I didn't hear 'em till just as my master called, and my room is over yours."

"I was awake," said Eleanor. She came up to the table, and even when answering, did not take her eyes off Adam, who cowered beneath them visibly.

"If you please, sir, to let me go on," said the policeman, "for this is serious. You could swear to the man, you say?"

"Yes—I could."

" He had no crape on, then?"

" No ; he had a red wig and beard, and they fell off in the scuffle."

" Shepherd, take my lantern, and just you run down to the spot, and look everywhere for a beard and wig. If they are found, we shall have a clue. Now then, when his beard and wig fell off, what was he like?"

Adam tried not to see Eleanor's eyes, but they fascinated him. He twisted and groaned as if with pain ; and said he could only just see he had dark hair. There was a moon then, and he could see that.

" Adam," asked Mr. Clavering, " do you believe it was the German ?"

" I am sure of it, sir."

" Did you suspect him before?"

" Yes, sir, I must say I did. He looked too knowingly got up to be real."

The policeman turned quietly, and gave the speaker a side glance, that seemed to say,

" You are up to that, are you? Well," he continued, aloud, "and the woman—what was she like ?"

He muttered something inaudible, and complained of being faint.

" Have you any salts, Mrs. Mornay?" asked Mr. Clavering.

She knew where some were always kept for Arthur, and hastened to offer them. Adam held out his hand, and as it touched hers, gave her fingers an unobserved gripe, and then looked at her keenly.

" Did *you* hear them, ma'am?   I was afraid you were disturbed."

She made no answer; only became paler.

" Did you hear anything before I did, Mrs. Mornay?" asked Mr. Clavering.

She was still silent, and still kept her eyes on Adam.

" Don't you hear my master speaking to you, ma'am?" put in Nurse Moyle. "And may I ask, too, if you have been to bed at all to-night, for it strikes me you have not."

She was, indeed, in the dress she had worn that evening, only a close observer might have seen the skirts were torn and wet. The policeman *was* a close observer, and he noted it at once.

" I did not go to bed," she replied, as if it was a relief to be able to answer.

" Did you think so badly of poor Arthur ?" said Rupert.

" No; he seemed easier when I left him."

At this moment, the shepherd came back with the wig and beard. There could be no doubt whose they were. The policeman took them into his keeping. "We must get out a warrant against the party, whether German or not. He cannot be far off, if he was badly wounded. My notion is, he is an old hand at this work."

" What work ?" asked Eleanor.

" Burglary, ma'am. You don't know, perhaps, that we brought a sack of plate in with
us, that we picked up by the summer-house.
It will be easily seen if it belongs to the
family."

The plate was brought forward, and identi-
fied. It was not what was under Adam's care,
but some that had been recently bought, and
was kept in a chest of which Miss Clavering
had the key.

" You had my niece's keys last night, Mrs.
Mornay," said Rupert. " Did you notice if
the plate-chest key was among them ?"

She felt in her pocket immediately, and pro-
duced the bunch. The key was there.

" Run up, nurse, and see if the lock has
been tampered with."

Nurse Moyle went, and returned with the
news that the chest had been emptied, but the
lock seemed all right.

" You did not give these keys out of your
own keeping, Mrs. Mornay, did you ?"

" No, sir."

" You locked up that money of mine, did you not ?"

" Yes, sir," interrupted Adam, " I saw her do it."

" You saw her? How came you to be there ?"

" Mrs. Mornay had been speaking about that party at the Lion, you know, sir, that you saw me talking to; who asked so much about the German—and I thought it would ease her mind if I stepped there to make inquiry, so I followed her to ask."

" Were you uneasy about that person last night, Mrs. Mornay ?"

She made a slight sign of assent. The policeman eyed her, and then Adam, but did not seem disposed to interrupt. Nurse Moyle, who had, meanwhile, come close to the lady, now took hold of her dress. " What ever have you been adoing, ma'am? Here is a great piece torn out of your gown, and you are quite wet.

And what is this stain on your sleeve? It is blood—what have you been about?"

The policeman came up, and looked at her dress closely. "Perhaps this belongs to you, ma'am. I picked it up on the grass."

It was a fragment of the same material, matching exactly. She knew in a moment that she must have torn it off in her fall. A gulf seemed opening under her feet, the very sight of which made her head dizzy.

"You are quite certain sure, *now*," said the policeman to Adam, "that you couldn't swear to the woman you saw?"

Adam turned and looked at him, then at his master, then at Nurse Moyle; and all three followed his eyes as he slowly fixed them on Eleanor.

"I am not so sure as I was, but my head is so bad, I can't think. Oh dear, oh dear, Mr. Clavering, sir, can you do nothing for this pain?"

"We must get you to bed, my poor fellow,

and as soon as it is daylight, we will have the doctor. The policeman will, perhaps, be kind enough to send him."

" I beg your pardon, sir, but I must not leave the house. Would you step this way a minute, sir—I want to speak to you."

Rupert Clavering took up a candle, and walked with him into the next room.

" What is it? You do not surely be-lieve——"

" Look here, sir. It is no time to mince words. It lies between them two. One or the other, or both, are concerned in this night's work, and the question is, which is to be believed most. How long has he been with you ?"

" Seven years."

" Where did you hire him?"

" Ah, poor fellow—that is not in his favour. It was on ticket-of-leave, in Australia. He was pardoned for his good conduct, and has been a capital servant."

"Ticket-of-leave, and pardoned. And the lady?"

" She is Miss Clavering's companion and friend. We have known her partially for some months."

" Do you know her history—where she comes from ?"

" I am sorry to say I do not."

" Then I am sorry to say, sir, I must do my duty. I must watch them both. You send them to bed, and take care they don't leave their rooms. I don't want to be uncivil, but you see I am responsible."

" I would stake my life on her innocence. She is the sweetest, gentlest creature in the world."

" Maybe, sir; but she may have had bad companions, for all that. They can't always help themselves, poor souls. Was any property in her keeping ?"

" No; she only locked up that money for me last night. In this desk, I think."

" Just see if it is there."

Rupert Clavering opened the desk. The pocket-book was gone. He felt so sick he could hardly stand.

" This is ugly," said the policeman, " but keep all quiet. Don't frighten her—only make her go to her room, and don't let her leave it. If she is reasonable, I will be civil; and if she will confess, so much the better ; but she must be told all she says will be made a note of. That is only fair."

Mr. Clavering had ridden for his life across a country on fire, but did not tremble then as he did now. He went first to Nurse Moyle—gave her some directions in a low voice, and then took Eleanor's hand. " Come, Mrs. Mornay, you must go to bed. Now, do not say anything more—I insist upon it—I ask it as a favour. Do, I implore you, go up quietly, and promise not to leave your room till you are called."

" I cannot, sir—I cannot go to bed. Oh, Mr. Clavering !"

"Hush, hush—come here; I want to speak to you." He took her into the passage, and grasped her by both hands. "You are not guilty, I know."

"Oh, God forbid! I saw you were all suspecting me; and yet how could you believe it?"

"I don't—I won't—and yet, I cannot help appearances. That money, you know——"

"Here it is. I hope it is all safe."

He took it mechanically, dismayed beyond the power of speech.

"I wouldn't believe the policeman," he said, at last. "Will you tell me the truth before I leave you? I have not a moment to spare."

"Oh, let me see Miss Clavering!"

"Anne? No, indeed. She is too unwell. I am only anxious to prevent her being disturbed. Mrs. Mornay, I would spare you anything I could, but I can do nothing, if you will not spare yourself. If you would not be in actual custody, you must go to your room, and

Nurse Moyle must see that you do not leave it."

" Oh no, sir—not till I have spoken to Miss Clavering. Oh, sir, have pity upon me—do not send me up-stairs. If I only dared to tell you all——"

The policeman opened the door into the passage, and stood quietly looking at them. " I'm going to see your man snug in bed, sir; and this good lady will do the same by Mrs. Mornay, if agreeable to you."

Nurse Moyle came out as he spoke, and put her hand, not unkindly, on Eleanor's shoulder.

" Come you to bed, and don't make more noise than you can help. No one is going to hurt you; you needn't shiver like that."

" Oh, Mrs. Moyle, Mrs. Moyle—for one minute, let me speak to Miss Clavering!"

" Not for your life. She is asleep, I hope, and I'll not wake her for anybody. You will see her in the morning, if she is well enough. Come now, be a sensible woman, and do as you are bid, for there is no help for it, and all this only makes it worse."

She drew her arm in hers, and half carried her up the stairs. Eleanor offered no more resistance, but seemed incapable of exerting herself, and when in her own room, sank down on the floor with her face hidden against the bed-clothes. No entreaty could make her rise, or undress; and Nurse Moyle was obliged to leave her, and content herself with securing the door outside.

Arthur Sydney, worn out with pain, had slept, off and on, rather longer than usual. He woke between four and five, thirsty and faint, and longing for his early cup of milk; but patiently resolved not to disturb anybody before the time; and was wishing he could go to sleep again and forget it, when he thought he heard a sound in the next room, as if some one was moaning in pain. Mrs. Mornay was his next neighbour, and as he had often said, she never seemed to move a finger from the time she went into her room till she came out, so this was something quite new. He listened —sat up in bed—and became so convinced of the fact, he knocked with his stick against the wall.

" What's amiss ? Can I ring up anybody ?"

There was a cry in return, as of intense relief. " Captain Sydney ! can you hear me ?"

" Not well," he shouted—" try the door."

There was a door between their rooms, but it was kept locked on her side, and a piece of furniture was against it on his. He heard her unfasten it, and her voice became more audible.

" Captain Sydney, can you help me ? Can you help me ?"

" What is it, my dear lady ? Are you ill ? Let me ring for assistance."

" I am not ill, but I am almost in despair. I want to speak to Miss Clavering, and they will not let me, and I shall go mad if they keep me here. It is a case of life and death.

Captain Sydney, for the sake of all you ever loved, keep your promise to me last night; do not mind what you hear, or what they tell you, but help me to five minutes with Miss Clavering, and I shall bless you as long as I live !"

"Why don't you go, and speak to her in her room ?"

"They have locked me in. The house has been robbed, and they think I helped to do it."

"They do ? then here goes ;" and he rang his bell fiercely. There was a longer delay than usual; he rang again: Nurse Moyle presently appeared, with his tumbler of new milk.

"Put that down, nurse, and go and unlock Mrs. Mornay's door. What do you mean by treating her so ?"

"Ah, my dear, it is not my fault, and she knows it. I am sorry for her, but it must be done."

"You are killing her among you! She is quite ill with agitation, and she implores a word with Miss Clavering. Will you let her know, or must I?"

"Now, Captain, do you think I am going to have her woke up, and she so ill, too?"

A bell rang at that moment.

"There now, that was your doing, sir. You rang so loud, you startled her, poor dear. We shall have her with a headache again all day."

"Mrs. Moyle," implored Eleanor, from her room, "are you there?"

"Yes, ma'am."

"Will you take a message to Miss Clavering now?"

"What is it, if you please?" Nurse Moyle was beginning to relent, and to feel misgivings about the justice of her severity.

"Will you tell her that I entreat her to come to me, as soon as possible, only for five minutes—entreat her on my knees. I know she will not refuse me."

" Well, Mrs. Mornay, as she is awake, I will
see what I can do.   I will promise this, at any
rate—if you will keep quiet, and not worret
yourself or the Captain, while I make her a
cup of tea, I will take it in to her, and see how
she is.   If she is pretty well, I will tell her all
about it, and give your message; if I find her
poorly and low, I shall just coax her to go to
sleep again, let who will beg and pray.   Now,
be satisfied with that, for I can promise nothing
more."

It seemed a long time, even to Sydney, before any sign was given of the promise being
kept.   Eleanor obeyed the injunction so far as
not to appeal to him again, but he heard her
walking up and down her room as if she could
not keep still; and it put him in a fever of impatience and sympathy.   He was never more
thankful than when at last a light step in the
passage, and the turning of the key in the
lock, announced the arrival of Miss Clavering.

Anne had awoke refreshed, her headache gone, and her spirits a little revived; and she was on the alert directly Nurse Moyle began her story. But the message, and the intimation that Mrs. Mornay was suspected, excited her so much, her old friend was more alarmed than by her previous languor. She hardly spoke, but dressed herself in haste, and went straight to the prisoner's room, as if afraid her courage would fail her if she delayed a moment to think.

Eleanor turned on her entrance, looked at her, but stood still. The agony expressed in every feature moved Anne's compassion strongly; she came up to her with her hand extended.

"You were quite right to send for me. You knew I would see you had justice."

"It is not so much your justice I would appeal to, as your mercy. Miss Clavering, I sent for you to give you—what I refused you once."

She held out the bracelet. Anne recoiled—
the blood surging up to her temples. "What
do you mean by that?"

"I have kept my promise—I have only just
discovered from whom it came—I return it to
its owner."

She put it into Anne's passive hand, and
before she could stop her, had fallen on her
knees at her feet.   ·

"For Heaven's sake!" gasped Anne, trying
to make her rise. "I beseech you, Mrs. Mornay——"

She looked up; their eyes met, and all was
told. Anne covered her face with her hands,
and leaned for support against the table.

"It was only this night," said Eleanor, still
kneeling, "that I learned what I now know;
this night, that has been such a terrible one,
and may have such terrible consequences,
unless you are what I believe you to be. I
know how you have been wronged. I know
who wronged you. I know what I must be

in your eyes—and I am here at your feet, to implore your pardon—to tell you there is but one hope for us now in our utter extremity, and that hope is in *you*."

Anne's hand dropped; she looked down at her suppliant as if alarmed for her reason. But Eleanor seized the hand now within her reach, and held it in both her own.

"Think," she went on, "who it is that kneels to you—think what it must be to address you thus—think what I have suffered—what we have all suffered together—and if ever you have cherished a bitter feeling against one who injured you without knowing it, let this humble posture make some small atonement, and win your pardon for that bitter wrong, whose shadow has fallen on us both!"

"Oh, say no more, say no more, Mrs. Atterbury—you make me too unhappy. You must not kneel like this! I will do anything for you, if you will stand up!"

"Not yet—not yet!" she said, clinging

faster, the calmness she had hitherto pre-
served by an effort, giving way before the
pressure of her fears, "you have not heard all
—you do not know what I am going to entrust
to you—more than my life—more than my honour—he is at this moment hid in your house."

"What?—Who?—Your husband?"

"Yes—behind the secret panel. He bade
me meet him in the garden—you will forgive
me that—I had not spoken to him for two
years; and while we were in the summer-
house, Adam came there with a bag of plate,
and they had a struggle when he saw he was
found out, and he recognised Frederick—and
wounded him with his knife, and Frederick
knocked him down, and then carried me in,
for I had fainted. He had lost a great deal of
blood, and I had just tied up his arm, when
we heard people outside, bringing Adam home,
and he implored me to hide him, and I had
nowhere else. And there he is, helpless and
faint, dying perhaps, and I could not persuade

them to let me speak to you—the only one I dared trust. They think I went to meet the German artist, and I was obliged to bear it, for fear Adam should let out whom he had seen, and they shut me up here, and I thought you would **never come—and he,** all this while——"

And here she broke down utterly, and sank weeping on **the** floor.

At that sight, at those words, the spirit of bitterness fled from Anne Clavering, never to return. All her own generous self was restored in renewed vigour and warmth, as she raised the crushed sufferer from the ground, laid her, now almost exhausted, on her bed, and by tender touch and gentle words, tried to expiate the harshness that she could not bear to remember.

" Listen to me, my poor friend," she said, as she bent over **her,** and held her hand in hers, " we have no **time** now for more than a few words, but these I *must* say. When I sent you that wedding gift, it was in an evil spirit, for

which I, in turn, ask your pardon.   I thought
it would be a joy to know that you would ever
suffer half I had gone through.   And now I
would give all I have to save you.   Forget
how it was sent you then, as I would pray
God to forgive it.   Take it once more as my
gift; it is to you it should belong; take it as a
proof that you too can forgive, and as a pledge
of the promise I solemnly make you here, that
as a sister I will stand by you—as a sister I
will act and think for you both; and God do
so with me and mine as I deal with you!"

"Oh, may He bless you—may He reward
you—may He give you tenfold for this!" said
Eleanor, as she raised herself on the bed, and
flung her arms round Anne's neck. "Go, go—
I trust you as I would an angel, for it is an
angel's work to rejoice in repentance, and his
is as bitter as his doom!"

Anne Clavering returned the embrace, but
she could trust herself to say no more.   Her
heart was full, and she required a moment to

think, to consider what was to be done first. She stood still, after leaving the room, holding her hand to her brow, and debating in whom she had better confide first, when, to her extreme relief, Edward Wilton appeared, coming softly up-stairs with his bag in his hand, looking very much as if he had travelled all night.

"Why, what is the matter with you all?" he said. "I expected you would all be in bed, or very like it; and here is the whole house turned upside down. I came by the night train, and waited till I thought I might venture to walk over. Did I startle you?"

"Never mind—I have no time to think of that. Dear Edward, you are always my help and comfort; you do not know how welcome you are at this moment. Come here."

She opened Eleanor's door; Eleanor, who was listening for every sound, sprang to meet her. "What is it?"

"My cousin is arrived; you could not have a kinder or a better adviser. Will you trust him?" And, hardly waiting for leave, she dragged Wilton in "Edward, this lady is one you have often felt for—you will feel for her now. This is Mrs. Atterbury. Stay"— for the colour rushed to his cheeks, as he looked from one to the other in amazement— "we cannot wait to explain; every moment is precious; only this—that she has shown a generous trust in me, and I have promised to stand by her. Will you help me to keep the promise, and stand by us both?"

The earnestness of the one, the distress of the other, showed him that this was indeed a time for actions, not words. He hastened to assure them of his readiness and zeal to serve a lady he respected so highly as he did Mrs. Atterbury; gave her hand the cordial shake which, with an Englishman, stands in the place of vow and protestation, and then obeyed Anne's eager summons outside. As soon as they were alone, she hurriedly explained the true state of the case.

He saw the peril in a moment. "How long has he been there?"

"Some hours at least. You do not think there is danger in that?"

"Not danger exactly, but punishment enough —even for him. Let me just say that much, and I will do all a man can do to bring him off—if only for the sake of that poor young wife. Come down, and let us see if we can get into the hall."

They went down cautiously, but a terrible disappointment awaited them. The hall was occupied already, and as they opened the door, they heard voices in eager consultation, and the well-known whine of old Bruno. Anne understood the meaning of this directly.

"Oh, Edward!" she whispered, drawing back, "*the dog has found him out!*"

They exchanged a look of consternation; for a moment, almost of despair. He held up his finger, and they stood in the doorway, unnoticed by the others, now gathered round

Bruno, intently watching his movements. The policeman had been joined by his superintendent and another, and Uncle Rupert, and Thomas, and two of the maids, were all there, and all equally perplexed by the dog's excitement. He snuffed at the wall, and whined, and scratched, as if he would tear it open.

" Is there anything behind these panels, sir ?" the superintendent asked Uncle Rupert ; a question that made both cousins hold their breath with anxiety.

" Rather curious that you should suggest such a thing," was the reply, "for the fact is, I know there used to be a closet in this hall with a secret spring ; but I never saw it, and could not tell you which panel it is. There was a sad story connected with it, which led to its being disused, and forgotten."

" Well, sir, it strikes me somebody knows more about it than you do. With your leave, I should like to try if this panel can be opened."

He rapped it with his stick as he spoke.

Bruno scratched harder than ever, and set up a long howl.

" Edward," whispered Anne, "if they break in, he may do something mad. He is armed, and desperate. I must tell them the truth, and open the door."

" He may fire at you by mistake."

" I am not afraid. He will know my voice —the only one he does know here. There is no help for it now; they must see him, and the only chance is to face it boldly."

He saw she was right, if she had only nerve to play her part. There was no time for debate; the police were examining the chimney and panelling to make sure where the attempt should be made, and they were not a little surprised when Miss Clavering stepped forward, observing with a smile that she could save them a great deal of trouble, by explaining the whole mystery. In the first place, the closet had been discovered by Mr. Wilton—and in the second, she knew the gentleman who was hid in it at the present moment. Bruno was quite right—he recognised his old friend. "Your photographer, uncle, proves to be an old acquaintance of ours, but having fallen into adversity, he came in that disguise, hoping no one would recognise him—his only object being to obtain an interview with his wife."

"His wife? Mrs. Mornay?"

"Yes. She has just told me everything. She will tell *you*, now that she is no longer terrified on his account. Uncle, this gentleman was a favourite of Uncle Henry's—he used to be constantly here—he ought to have known better than to hide himself from his friends. I am sure you will give him a kind reception, especially when you hear that in trying to save your house from robbery, he nearly lost his life."

The police exchanged a few words, and looked significantly at Mr. Clavering, who seemed too much shocked to speak.

"I see," said Anne, turning to the superintendent, to whom she was personally known, "you understand now, Mr. Redlands, where to look for the true culprit. Adam, being discovered by this gentleman in the act of carrying off the plate, attempted, first, to silence him with his knife, and then to shift his guilt on his shoulders. You will hear the full particulars later; the thing to be done now, is to release our innocent guest."

She made a sign to Wilton, who opened the door. A ghastly figure staggered out, blinded by the rush of light, and exhausted with loss of blood. He almost fell into a chair, gasping an entreaty for water. It was brought, and Anne, motioning the others back, put it to his lips, and bathed his forehead. His eyes closed heavily, and he drew long sighs of faintness, but the air and water reviving him a little, he lifted his head, and looked at her with a mournful earnestness that nearly overcame her resolution.

"You know where you are, do you not?"

she said, cheerfully, so that all might hear, while she pressed her finger on his hand in sign of caution. "You remember this room, and old Bruno? He remembers you, at any rate," as the dog came snuffing about his knees, "and if he could speak, he would tell you, it was a very ungenerous thing to hide yourself from your old acquaintance in your adversity. You deserve a worse punishment even than what you have had."

"I do, indeed, Miss Clavering," murmured he, "and yet it has been very heavy. Are those men waiting to take me up?"

"Are you, Mr. Redlands?" she asked, turning to the superintendent with a smile; "can we prosecute him for burglary, do you think?"

"Not exactly, Miss Clavering; I am sure I am very sorry you have been so disturbed and annoyed; but I do say, it was not a sensible thing for any gentleman to do, and might have led to very unpleasant consequences. I would advise you, sir, never to do such a thing again."

Atterbury shuddered involuntarily. " It was the nearest approach to being buried alive I ever thought to see. How long was I there ?"

" What time did you go in, sir ?"

" It was about three."

" And it is now seven. Nigh upon four hours."

" Only four hours ! It might have been twenty for their length. But I have my own cowardice to thank. My wife begged me to trust to Mr. Clavering's goodness, and—I had not the courage."

" Sir," said Uncle Rupert, who had not spoken till now, but who felt his hospitality appealed to here, " any one whom my brother received, must be welcome to me—still more, when introduced by my niece. I only wish you had taken your amiable wife's advice, as you would not only have escaped all this suf-fering yourself, but have spared her considerable distress.   I owe her a thousand apologies for having doubted her for a moment.   Step this way, Redlands, will you?"   He drew the superintendent aside.   " This is a strange business, certainly, but there can be no doubt as to the fact. I was wrong to trust so much to that miserable fellow—the blame rests on me. I see now, he must have had skeleton keys, to enable him to open any lock in the house, and that man whom I told you I had seen him talking to, may have been his accomplice."

" Not much doubt of that, Mr. Clavering, if he is the party I think he is. We are on his traces, and are pretty sure of the mark."

" Well, it is a weight off my mind, at any rate, that that poor lady is cleared. Try and keep all this from getting into the papers, Redlands, if you can. As to that wretched man up-stairs, we must see; I don't wish to prosecute; and he is too ill to be questioned at present; but I shall be glad if you will let Mr. Wynne know, and ask him to step up here at his leisure. Let your men have some break-fast, while we get this gentleman to bed. The quieter he is kept, the better, till the surgeon comes."

The civil superintendent made no objections; he might have his own opinion, but he kept it to himself, and having spoken to his men, who had been examining the closet with the zest of antiquarians, withdrew with them to be feasted by the servants, while they talked over the extraordinary adventure. Old Thomas, however, lingered behind the rest, peering at Atterbury with his hand over his eyes, to assist the failing vision which he had begun to doubt. No one observed him, as Mr. Clavering and Edward were busy with their guest, who had sunk back in his chair, in an attitude of deep dejection and languor.

"Take heart, sir," said Rupert, kindly, "your dangers are over, I hope; you are among friends."

"Am I?" he repeated, slowly. "Friends

here? Well, I must bear it—I deserve it all. Miss Clavering spoke the truth—I hoped not to be known—but since I am, I must accept your kindness. No, no!" with a sudden revulsion of feeling, that for the moment restored his energy, "I cannot—I must not! Call those fellows back—tell them everything—let them claim the reward—anything sooner than be kindly treated here again, and feel all the time, even that old man knows the wretch that I am!"

"Silence, sir!" said Anne, in a tone that had instantaneous effect, "for your wife's sake —your loving, devoted wife, who has been exposed this very night to disgrace and misery for yours—command yourself for a few minutes. Think of her, if you would have others think of you, and let us all agree in making her our first consideration. Come," she went up to him, and took his arm, "my cousin will support you, and I will show you your room. The sooner you are safely there the better.

Uncle, if you will wait here for me, I will come back to you directly."

Passively as a child, Atterbury submitted to her orders, and Rupert waited patiently for her return. He would not even question Thomas, who, shaking his head, and muttering to himself, withdrew to his own region. The interval was rather longer than she had promised, and when she came back, she flew into his arms, and hid her face. "Uncle Rupert, dear Uncle Rupert, forgive me."

"For what, my love? If you mean for keeping this discovery of yours a secret, do not vex yourself about it for a moment. I own I think secrets are foolish things, but it is of very little consequence. What I want to know, is about this gentleman; who is he, that he should be afraid to be known, and what was his position when you knew him before?"

"Who is he?—what was he?—what he never can be again. Uncle, forgive me, if I

even seemed to be trying to deceive you; it
was only to save him, as I promised to do.
His wife trusted me, and I will redeem the
trust, and you will be the first to bid me do
it." She clung to him as she did the first day
of his arrival, and he felt how strongly she
was agitated. The truth flashed upon him.

" Anne, my child—it is impossible—even *he*
could not be so utterly devoid of shame——"

She lifted her face. " Devoid of shame, did
you say? Did you ever see a man more
crushed by it? I never did; I hope I never
shall. Oh, uncle, we may forgive him now!
You would, if you remembered him as I do,
and saw how he is changed!"

" He deserves to suffer," said Rupert,
sternly.

" Perhaps so; but what are we that we should
judge each other? Uncle, hear me—I have
something I must tell you while I can; in your
arms I am strong enough for anything—even
for this, which may lose me some of your love.

You know how ill you thought me on your
birthday; it was on that day I found out who
Mrs. Mornay was—found it out through a
token which *he* gave me, and which, in the
bitterness of my heart, I sent her the day
before her marriage—the day you came home.
She did not suspect I had discovered her, and
I kept my secret, but an evil spirit seemed to
get possession of me, when I thought of all I
had suffered through her, and that all the right
in him had passed from me for ever, and was
hers, hers only—I cannot tell you how I
hated her. Oh, what dreadful hours I had,
when you all thought it was only my nerves
and headache—and she so gentle and sweet-
tempered with me all the while, that I hated
myself every time I had given her a harsh
word, as I did too often. And just now, when
she sent for me in her sore distress, to tell me
she knew all, and to throw herself and him on
my mercy—when I saw her kneeling and praying to me, knowing what she knew, and yet

trusting me in spite of all—I would have died
to make her happy—I would now, to save and
cheer them both.   More, I would live to see
it, and be glad in it, if God will let me.   Have
I not blessings enough in the love that is given
me, to keep me from selfish repinings, for that
which I have not ?   Uncle, say that you forgive me ; and for my sake help me to keep the
promise I have made—to be a sister to Atterbury's wife !"

He folded her tighter to his bosom; he
pressed his lips on her forehead; and she knew
that her petition was granted, though at the
cost of a struggle very nearly as hard as her
own.

CHAPTER II.

HOW MRS. ATTERBURY LOST HER BRACELET.

IT was not to be expected that such an event as this should not cause a sensation, not only in the village, but in the whole neighbour- hood. Such strange reports were circulated, that people were constantly coming from all parts to look at the outside of the house with the secret chamber, even if they could pene- trate no farther; and, in spite of Mr. Clavering's endeavours, the accounts in the papers were glowing and graphic in proportion to the scan-

tiness of the real information. The first visitor
was the old Vicar, Mr. Wynne, who, being a
family friend, and a magistrate, was almost the
only one who was welcome. His advice and
support were of great consequence under the
circumstances, for the police, though uniformly
civil, were anything but satisfied, and kept a
quiet watch upon the house and its inmates,
that deprived them of all feeling of security.
Adam was, or appeared to be, too ill from his
blow, to be examined; and they were glad to
keep him in bed, and prevent his finding out
what had taken place; but after hearing the
policeman's report, Mr. Wynne saw it would
be expedient for her own safety to take the
evidence of the lady, and after talking it over
with Mr. Clavering, a message was sent up to
request the favour of Mrs. Mornay's presence.
Atterbury, by whose bed she was sitting when
the message was given, turned at the mention

of the Vicar's name.   "Ask him to come up here."

He came, little knowing whom he should see, for the Claverings had not felt at liberty to divulge the secret; and hardly could he believe his own eyes, when they fell on the changed face, which had been so radiant with health and animation when he saw it last. The recollection of his past conduct made even the good old man's blood boil, and he stopped short in the middle of the room, as if almost indignant at such a meeting being forced upon him.

" I do not wonder at your hesitation," said Atterbury, after a short silence; "you must think I am hardened indeed, if I can bear to face an old friend, and to be seen by him here.   But I have no choice, and I have another to think for.   Mr. Wynne, this is my wife."

The Vicar turned to Eleanor, who had risen
to give him her chair, and grasped her hand
with silent energy. She looked appealingly in
his face, and drew him nearer the bed. "He
has suffered so much—he has so much still to
suffer—do not be harsh with him!"

Mr. Wynne could not resist her; he allowed
himself to be seated, and addressed the wounded
man gravely, but not unkindly.

"You wished me to come to you, Mr. Atterbury—why?"

"Because, if my wife has to answer your
questions, it was necessary you should know
the whole truth. She will tell you now whatever you require to hear."

To be allowed to tell the whole truth was
all Eleanor wanted, and in as few words as she
could, she put the Vicar in possession of all the
facts. Atterbury explained that Adam owed
him a grudge, for having detected his thefts

when in his father's service, and that his principal danger now lay in his giving information of his being in England. Even if he forbore to do so, yet if he were brought to justice, and they had to give evidence, the exposure would be equally fatal.

"The presence of mind of Miss Clavering saved me this morning, but nothing could do so a second time. As far as I am concerned, I have become so weary of being hunted about, I could almost take my chance; but here is one, Mr. Wynne, who, innocent from first to last, has already borne more than the guilty; and if I now accept the mercy of those I have wronged, it is more for her sake than my own."

"No one can help feeling for Mrs. Atterbury," said Mr. Wynne, watching her as she bent over her husband in silence, raising his pillow, giving him drink, and then sitting

down on the bed, that he might rest against
her shoulder. All the horror of the night
was past, and though her movements betrayed
her fatigue, there was a quiet hopefulness in
her eye and smile that told of inward peace
and trust, made stronger by deliverance. The
Vicar looked, and mentally resolved, that
come what might, her husband must be
brought off, somehow, even if he suffered for
abetting it.

"This must have been a terrible night for
you, Mrs. Atterbury."

"It was," she said, shivering at the remembrance. "I was almost in despair at one time,
but I was wrong. I have always found help
when it came to the worst, and I did then.
And if more trouble is in store for us, we shall
find it still. I am not afraid."

Her husband gave her a look, such as she
had often pined for in vain; and then whis-

pered a few words which the Vicar could not hear. She pressed her lips on his forehead, and left them together, and Mr. Wynne, taking Atterbury's hand, invited him to look upon him as a friend.

It was one of those moments, he saw, which if seized and employed, give colouring to the whole of the future life: the sight of the kind features—the sound of the friendly voice, had filled the unhappy young man's heart almost to overflowing; and the anguish of repentance and sorrow craved the relief of humiliation and confession. A wasted youth—an existence of self-indulgence—the miseries he had helped to cause—the deceits, the wrongs in which he had been gradually drawn to share—rolled over his spirit like an overwhelming tide, and his cry was that of the drowning, " Save me, or I perish !" And with such a case no one was fitter to deal than the experienced, kind-hearted counsellor into whose hands he had been thrown.

Brought up as he had been in the expectation of a large fortune, with little or no training for its management, encouraged to pass his youth, first in thoughtless pleasure, then in reckless dissipation, Atterbury had found himself, when he became a man, so burdened with debts and liabilities as to leave him helpless at the mercy of his father, and still worse, of those who held his father in their power. Of that father he could hardly bear to speak, but Mr. Wynne knew enough of the facts to divine much that was left unsaid. Only by slow degrees was the terrible state of their affairs revealed to the young partner; and the more he discovered, the more fearful he grew of further revelations, and the more desperate about himself. One thing he soon decided upon—that his union with Miss Clavering was utterly impossible. He could not wed her to ruin and disgrace; and all he could hope was, that by seeming to have become indifferent, he might teach her indifference too. His own happiness being wrecked, and his self-respect with it, he had at last sullenly submitted to be disposed of as his father and advisers wished; and then his punishment took a new form. He soon found what the woman was whose heart he was winning on false pretences; and the more she rose in his estimation, the more miserable he became at the fate he was bringing upon her. His voice and courage failed when he began on this topic, and it was some time before he could go on. Indeed, his whole narration was too broken and interrupted to be given literally, and the reader, who knows a good deal that the Vicar had to be told, will be satisfied with a brief summary of facts.

Mr. Martock's influence over the elder Mr.
Atterbury had by this time become a tyranny,
not the less keenly felt for his being, nominally,
his dearest friend, and confidential adviser.
What he decided upon, was to be done at all
costs, and Frederick's resistance, impetuous at
first, gradually changed into an outward submission, covering the deepest resentment and
hate. Night after night, during his father's
last illness, as he watched by his bedside, it
wrung his heart to see the terror haunting
even his sleep—the agony in which he would
start up to clasp his son's hand, and implore
him, if he valued his peace or his blessing, not
to thwart Martock's will, but to be guided by
his advice in everything. " So long as he is
our friend, we are safe—if he turns against us,
we are lost!" was the cry that rang in the
young man's ears long after the voice that
uttered it was still; and it influenced him

more than he was aware. The father's death did nothing to free the son. His papers revealed nothing of the secret that had made him a slave; and the closer insight Atterbury obtained of his affairs, only showed him a deeper gulf of ruin than he had believed in before. He was soon made to understand his position. If he would, as his father had done, submit to be ruled by his tyrant, all would go well for the present; his marriage would secure him wealth, under certain conditions, and time and help would be given for the settlement of his private, and the partial retrieving of his public affairs. If, on the other hand, he yielded to the impulse that made him long to proclaim the truth at all risks, then Mr. Martock would no longer have an object in keeping back what he had concealed hitherto; and Mr. Atterbury must take the consequences.

We know how he decided. And the decision made, and the yoke rivetted on his neck, he gave himself up to a desperate resolve not to investigate, not to interfere, not to know more than he could help, of what was going on in his name, and on his responsibility. While Martock and Despard, the two evil counsellors that he owed to his father, acted for him as they pleased, he accepted the part he was told was necessary—that of presenting a brilliant exterior in the sight of the world; and moved among a circle of admiring and envying friends, the object of his own scarcely disguised contempt. The one link that bound him to nobler and better thoughts, that kept him from feeling himself absolutely cut off from hope, was the attachment of Eleanor Ormonde, though his remorse on account of his conduct to her and Anne Clavering, embittered even that single drop of consolation.

Such was his state when he married—not knowing at what period, distant or near, the ruin would fall on their heads, but that come it must, and one man, when he pleased, could bring it on at any moment. His deception of his wife the day that he took her from Wardenstone to Twalmley, was not from heartlessness. Having passed his word to Mr. Martock that he would be in town that night, he yet shrank from the dreadful avowal to his unsuspecting bride, and desperately resolved she should know it from other sources, and he would, for the last time, give her a happy day. He did not know how dear she had become till that moment; if his blood could have atoned for the past, he would have poured it freely ; but he could not tell her the truth.

The whole truth was not known, even to himself; and the horror with which he learned that he was accused of fraud and swindling, rendering him liable to a criminal prosecution, made him listen willingly to Despard's advice, to fly; backed as it was by the hope that his absence would lighten the difficulties of his wife. How much he had been mistaken in this, we know already—and he had at last begun to realise; and it seemed almost hopeless that the devotion of a lifetime would be sufficient atonement.

It was a sad history, but told in this manner, it could not be listened to without pity; the old clergyman felt his magisterial severity melted in sorrow and regret; and versed in the human heart by long experience, he saw the deep remorse was real, the yearning for a new course sincere and humble. He hardly knew what to advise without further reflection, but he comforted and encouraged him to persevere, and promised when he left him, to see him again the next day.

" He has sinned heavily," he observed to Mr. Clavering, as he quitted the house, " but he has suffered for it, and will suffer more yet, if we do not take care. Keep him close, for we must get him away as soon as we can. If I do wrong in furthering his escape, I must take the consequences. I cannot see that poor young lady's heart quite broken."

" He is under my roof, sir," returned Mr. Clavering, gravely, " and that is pledge sufficient that all I can do for him shall be done."

The interview with Mr. Wynne, though it relieved Atterbury's mind, was rather too much for his strength, and the surgeon found him in such a feverish state, that he ordered him to be kept perfectly quiet for the remainder of the day. Towards the afternoon he fell into a refreshing sleep, during which Eleanor's friends urgently entreated her to do the same, as she

was even more exhausted than her husband.
The little room that had been hastily prepared
for him was just opposite hers, so that she
would be within hearing if she were wanted;
and Anne was so resolved upon it, that she
made her yield, and saw her safely into bed,
waiting upon her with a tender assiduity, that
spoke eloquently to Eleanor's heart. It had
been arranged that she should be called in the
evening, so as to attend on Frederick, if necessary, in the night. "Get all the sleep you
can," advised Miss Clavering, "or I shall not
let you be disturbed. I wish you were like
that wretched Adam. He has been asleep
nearly all day."

"Is that a good sign?"

"Well, the surgeon says he is going on well,
but he appears not to understand or hear what
is said to him. Just as well, perhaps, for himself and us. Now go to sleep. Edward is a

capital nurse, and while he takes care of your husband, I mean to watch over you."

" He has given his angels charge over us," whispered Eleanor, with a grateful smile; and Anne had not left her five minutes, before she was sleeping like a child.

She awoke, some hours later, so much refreshed, that no persuasion could prevent her rising and dressing herself, so as to resume her attendance on her patient. He was restless with pain and fever, and she would not leave him again. For the first part of the night she was kept constantly on the alert, but about one o'clock he fell into an uneasy slumber, and thence, by degrees, into more satisfactory repose. All was still in the house, and Eleanor, as she reclined in the chair by his bedside, began to feel her own eyes growing less watchful than she wished; till after two or three victories over the drowsiness, she woke up with a sudden start, almost forgetting where she was. In a moment, a strong hand was on her mouth, her wrists were grasped by another, and she found herself powerless in the gripe of Adam.

" Speak a word, or utter a sound, and I'll do for you both," he hissed in her ear; and so fierce was his gesture, so painful his grasp, she had little doubt he would keep his word. She had presence of mind enough to refrain from struggling, and to obey without resistance his menacing sign to come out of the room—thankful, even in her terror, to see him gently close the door on the unconscious sleeper. He took her into her own apartment, without releasing his hold, and having placed her in a chair, removed his hand from her mouth.

" If you speak above your breath, I shall have to stop it for you. Answer me in whispers, quick. You are his wife?"

" Yes."

" And you chose to risk his safety, sooner than your own. Hush, I know all about it. If you had kept my secret, I might have kept yours. Now I must take care of myself. What money have you got ?"

" I will give you my purse, if you will let go my hands."

" Look sharp, then." He released his hold, and she gave it up. " Mighty little here. Is this all you have ?"

" Yes, all."

" You have some diamonds, then; I know more than you think for."

" I had, but Mr. Wilton took them to town to dispose of."

" Has he given you the money ?"

" Not yet.   Indeed you may believe me."

" You had best tell me the truth, I know that. Where are your trinkets ?"

She gave him the key of her jewel-box. He seized the few ornaments she had left, including the bracelet, and then asked for her watch. "You are sure you have nothing more?"

"Nothing."

"Very well, this must do. Now, ma'am, I must tell you I am going to escape by your window, for the police are on the watch, and that is my only chance; but I'm not going to leave you to rouse the house before I can get clear away, so I must secure you first. I don't want to hurt you, but this *must* be done."

"Oh no, no, Adam—not that!" she pleaded, folding her hands in earnest supplication as he approached, "spare me that—my husband is too ill to be left—he might call me, and what should I do? Listen one moment, as he grasped her arm impatiently, "I will not rouse any one—I will do nothing—I will only go back and sit by his bed, and tell no one till the morning—I promise you faithfully, and I would not break my promise to save my life !"

"Well," he said, as if relenting in spite of himself, " perhaps you would not, but it is a risk. Here"— snatching up her small clasped Bible from the table—" swear it on this, and I'll see."

He thrust it to her lips; she kissed it reverently.

" Will that satisfy you ?"

" I suppose it must," he muttered, as he relinquished his hold; "and now, what will you give me in return ?"

" Give you? I would, but I have nothing left—nothing but this." She put the Bible into his hands. " Keep it in remembrance of having done a merciful action, and God forgive you all the rest !"

He shrugged his shoulders as he put the

book in his pocket, muttering something about all that coming too late now.

"Oh, do not say so!" she whispered, with a sudden impulse that she could not restrain; "you, who have been doing so well, who had such a fair prospect, whose master trusts and feels for you—it is not too late even now. Stop in time—I will do all I can for you, and so will he; even if you must suffer for a little while, better that, than give up all your hopes in this world and the next!"

"Tell your husband that," he returned, fiercely, "and see what he will say. Come! Every moment loses me a chance. I must see you back to his room. Mind now—if he wakes, and sees me, I'll settle you both."

He took her again by the arm, and they crossed the passage together in silence, and with noiseless steps. He opened Atterbury's door, signed to her to go in, and stood with it in his hand, watching. The sleeper had altered his position, and lay with his face towards his enemy, and his sound arm hanging down from the bed. As Eleanor approached, he moved; she stood still, her heart throbbing so that she could hardly breathe; he muttered something unintelligible, drew the clothes over his shoulder, and turned impatiently from the light. She waited a few moments, till she heard the door softly closed. She had just courage enough left to go and draw the bolt inside, and then resumed her seat by the bed, to watch and listen, and start at every sound, real or fancied—trying to be calm, to pray, to return thanks—but, in reality, able to do little more than sit shivering as if with ague, longing for the morning light, which seemed as if it would never come.

It would be impossible to describe the state of excitement and wrath into which the household of Lawleigh were thrown, when morning actually came, and they learned what had happened while they slept. The exasperation of Mr. Clavering, stung by the ingratitude of his protégé, and the disgrace inflicted on his hospitality, was only to be equalled by that of the police, though theirs was more guardedly expressed. They had watched the house in turn, all night, so that the escape of the thief must have been effected with an ingenuity that considerably raised his value in professional eyes. The open window in Eleanor's room showed where he had made his exit, though it was very provoking to think how very near he must have been to the sentinel, and that if an alarm could have been given, his arrest would have been certain. Of course, when a lady was forced to swear silence, she could not help herself; only, it was unfortunate. Not but what Mrs. Mornay did perfectly right in submitting; in short, no one could have behaved better; for if she had irritated him by resistance, there was no saying what he might have done. He had done quite enough, as it was, for though Eleanor commanded herself at first sufficiently to give a clear account of the whole affair, and answered all Mr. Wynne's questions about her lost property with tolerable composure, her nerves had been taxed too far, and she had not been left alone with Anne more than a few minutes, before she gave way to a burst of hysterical emotion, which she had no power to stop. With difficulty she was assisted to Miss Clavering's room—her own being occupied by the police—and Anne devoted herself to the task of calming and soothing her, but in vain: the sobs brought on a violent return of the cough, and the consequence was one long dreaded—the rupture of a blood-vessel.

Fortunately, the surgeon was in the house, and had just finished dressing Atterbury's wound, so that not a moment was lost, to which she might be said, in part, to owe her life, for even with all his care and skill, it hung on a thread for some hours. Her peril did what nothing else could have done—it broke down the barrier between Atterbury and his hosts; in his agony for his wife he forgot himself and them, and their pity for his grief, and their mutual anxiety about its object, swallowed up all other considerations. So trying to the sufferer, however, did his agitation become, that he was obliged to retire, and Mr. Wynne, from time to time, paid him visits, and did his best to keep him from despair. When at last she was out of immediate danger, and had fallen into a quiet sleep, Mr. Clavering went to see him, and found him alone, writing as well as he could, with his left arm in a sling, and looking wretchedly ill, and broken down. The kind-hearted man felt his heart swell with pity; and when Atterbury, rising, stood with downcast eyes, as if conscious how unworthy he was to be in his presence, he had to clear his throat, and recollect himself, before he could begin with the reserved politeness that he considered due to both.

" Now that we may hope that Mrs. Atterbury's danger is past, I am come, sir, to ask your pardon and hers, for having exposed her to such an outrage. I shall never forgive myself for not having taken proper precautions; but I was deceived all along; and, as you may suppose, I thought the rascal too ill to move. A description of the trinkets is in the hands of the police, as well as your photograph of the man, and I have offered a reward for the recovery of the property, so I have every hope it may be restored. I could pardon him anything but the shock to that delicate, gentle lady; and so could we all."

"You are very good, sir," said Atterbury, without raising his eyes, "and your goodness to her—only of a piece with what she has told me—is an obligation I *can* accept, without being crushed by shame."

"I hope so, sir, I hope so. It was impossible to know even the little we did of her, without regard and respect, and now, without the deepest sympathy and admiration. No, I shall never forgive myself—I ought to have protected her from this; but, sir, I did not believe that man was so bad—I had given him every chance—I had such hopes of him! Such a return is enough to harden one's heart; and yet, where you see repentance, how can you help trusting it? I always did, and I believe I always shall."

Atterbury looked up with a quick flush of

emotion. "Oh, if I might but think so!" But the shame was too strong, and sinking again into his seat, he laid his head on the table, covering his face with his arm.

It was not in Rupert Clavering's nature to strike the fallen, and this man was his guest, was overwhelmed with distress, and dependent on his generosity and kindness. His distress might be well deserved—he had little doubt it was—but it was as undeniable as his remorse and humiliation, and they were pleaders he never could resist. He came up to the table, and laid his hand on Frederick's shoulder.

"Mr. Atterbury, I do not pretend to be your judge; you best know of what your conscience has to accuse you; but if you are really a repentant man, all I can say is, God forbid that I, or any one belonging to me, should reject your repentance. From us you will hear no reproaches; I hope you will meet with

nothing but good will; we feel for your misfortunes, and we have a great regard for your
wife, and we will do our best to help you both
as far as you will allow us. If you are disposed to place any confidence in me, it shall
not be misplaced; I have some experience in
business, and what I have is at your service."

By a strong effort, the unhappy young man
raised himself from his dejected attitude, and
turned his face towards his companion. "Mr.
Clavering, I do not know what you may have
heard of me—what you may have thought—
but I know it must have been bad enough; I
have not a word to say against it; only this
you must try and believe, as you did of your
servant—I am not utterly lost to shame, not
entirely hardened in guilt. If I am here, it is
not because I have forgotten what I have
done; it is part of my punishment—the punishment that I have been enduring for years.

Drawn here by circumstances I could not foresee, it is now impossible for me to put the real truth from me, or to allow you to show me kindness, without offering you the one poor atonement that a man can offer, for wrong he can never repair, that of asking you, as I ask now,—will you forgive me?"

There was no mistaking the tone, the attitude in which this was asked; his humiliation was deep enough to have satiated revenge, and Mr. Clavering was pained to see it. He was too sincere, even in his courtesy, to imply that the wrong was light, or that the repentance needed to be transitory; but before he was aware, he had drawn a chair by the young man's side, and was talking to him gently, soothingly, encouragingly, giving him at least the comfort of seeing that his sorrow was accepted as real, and offering him practical advice for the future, which no one was better fitted to give. Atterbury's reserve melted before this unlooked-for kindness, and he showed his sense of it by frankly discussing his situation.

"Guilty as I am," he said, "of more than enough to deserve any punishment they please, of this particular crime with which I am charged, that of converting to my own use the deposits and securities of those parties who have offered so high a reward—I am as innocent as you are. If any such transaction took place, it was before my time. And having told you this, I must add further, that if I were guilty of all, I could not dread a trial more. If I could compound to take the penalty, and escape the horror of the investigation, I could almost do it thankfully. God help me if I have to go through it, for no one else can."

"Well, uncle," said Edward, meeting him

as he came out of the room, "what do you think?"

"I think, Ned, that Mr. Wynne is right, and I was wrong, as I often am. We must stand by this poor fellow now ; he has thrown himself on our mercy. I wish he was safely out of the country, but he will hear of nothing while his wife is in this state. Come, and let us consult the Vicar; for the case is serious, and we must be careful what we are about."

CHAPTER III.

HOW MRS. ATTERBURY RECOVERED HER BRACELET.

IT was in a very small house, in the north-west of London, whose rent, though low in comparison with others in better condition, was still heavy enough to weigh seriously on a very light purse, that Mrs. Tresham and her daughters had settled themselves at last, in the hope of adding to their income by taking pupils, or giving lessons. A great deal of discouragement and disappointment had been borne with a patience not quite unrewarded, for five or six little girls came regularly now to be taught as much as could be insinuated into their little unwilling brains by the exertions of Clara and Ellen; Mrs. Tresham, meanwhile, with the help of one maid-servant, keeping the house in order, and providing for the wants of every one. Her two younger boys had obtained presentations to public schools through her husband's City friends; and Charles Lyle had a curacy within four or five London miles, and came to cheer them up whenever he could, with visions of all he meant to do, when that Indian chaplaincy turned up, or that capital living fell to his share, which he always intended to have, but had not decided upon yet. There was much patient endurance in the little household; a good deal of cheerfulness in general, and, at times, a good deal of anxiety. One subject of care was rarely out of their minds; and this, the heaviest of all, was Herbert.

"Is not your brother dressed yet, Clara?" her mother asked one morning about this time, when, on returning to the small parlour from the kitchen, she found her daughter hovering about the deserted breakfast-table, trying to keep the tea hot, and putting cold meat temptingly ready for the late comer. "It is nearly time for your children, and it throws everything back when the things are kept so long."

It was a complaint that many mothers would have made sooner; but Clara knew too well how sorely her patience had been tried; and blushed as if the fault were hers.

"He will soon be down, I think; he sat up late, writing his novel, and that makes him tired in the morning, you know, mamma."

"Yes, dear, I do; but if he would rise early, he might work without burning so many candles, or hurting his health. I fear the novel will hardly repay the cost."

"Don't say so to him, dear mamma; it is his only comfort; and I am sure it must answer, when once it is finished; so clever as he is with his pen when he is in the vein, he must succeed. I am sure books come out every day that are not half as good."

"Perhaps so, love—but they are finished, you see." Mrs. Tresham sighed as she said this, and was turning to leave the room, when her son lounged in, his eyes heavy, his hair and dress in disorder, and looking only half awake. He stopped her with a kiss of assumed gaiety. "Finished, are they, mother? Not the pickles, I hope? How is your brew, Clara? I want it extra strong, I can tell you, for my head aches ready to split."

"You were late last night, then? Did you get much done?" asked his mother, putting his hair back from his hot forehead, as he took his seat.   She could murmur to Clara, but she had no heart to do so to *him*.

"Much done? Well, if I don't scratch it all out again, I believe I have turned a corner. It is grand work, mother, having a heroine who comes into a million of money, and pays all the hero's bills, with a stroke of her pen. I enjoy drawing cheques for enormous amounts so much, that if she has any luck, she will have to do it half a dozen times before he gives up his latch-key and repents. I say, Clara, this tea tastes—not like hay, that would be paying it too great a compliment—an old wisp of straw soaked in lukewarm water would be nearer the mark."

"Well, Herbert, if you had come down sooner, it would have been hotter, that is all I can say. You do not deserve any, it strikes me; for you promised yesterday——"

"I know, I know; but it *is* such a comfort to sleep. If I could, I would sleep all day. Never mind; when the book is done, I'll make it all up. A hundred pounds will be a jolly thing, mother, from your scapegrace boy? A hundred—a hundred and fifty at least; and more for a second edition. Indeed, I think I shall not let it go under three hundred. It is worth double the money."

"I dare say, dear; but you know you are only a beginner, so do not be too sanguine. Is there much to do?"

"Oh yes; and I must get a stretch this morning to refresh my wits for the grand crisis: I could not hit it off last night, and nearly put it all in the fire, in spite of the heroine's cheques. This beef is horribly tough, Clara. Couldn't you have ordered me a mouthful of something hot, with a dash of cayenne? That is what I fancy just now."

The mother and daughter exchanged a glance of sorrowful meaning. "My dear boy," Mrs. Tresham began, "if you would only consider a minute—it is more than we can well afford to go on as we do, and it is in these little things——"

"There, dear mother, I know all about it. It doesn't signify; if the table were covered with *entrées*, I should grumble that you had not given me something cold. It is my way, you know. Is the *Times* come yet?"

The *Times* was one of the luxuries that was included in Herbert's way, and he justified it to himself, by studying the advertisements diligently for that situation offering liberal salary, and other advantages, which, like Charles Lyle's capital living, was to turn up some day when you were not expecting it.

"Here it is for you, and an armful of letters into the bargain," said his sister; "but do finish your breakfast first, for we shall really want the room presently."

He shrugged his shoulders with impatience, and made a feint of drinking his tea in a hurry; but put down the cup half emptied, to tear open one envelope after another; his face growing gloomier with each experiment. When he had looked at the last, he crammed them all into his pocket; and affecting sublime indifference to their contents, again pretended to be doing great things in the way of breakfast. Clara was, meanwhile, glancing over the paper. Her leisure moments were few and valuable, but attendance on Herbert was a duty to which many others gave way, and though he was seldom in time for the family meals, he could not bear to take his own alone. She skimmed the columns without much heeding their purport, looking off perpetually to see if her brother was progressing as he ought, and almost wishing mamma would go, as she was sure by his face he had had unpleasant news, and was longing to pour it all out. But Mrs. Tresham was as quick-sighted as herself, and lingered on, in the hope that Clara's scholars would call her away, and leave her to receive the confidence that each tried to spare the other.

"Herbert! what is the name of Mr. Wilton's place in the country?" asked Miss Tresham, suddenly, after studying one corner of the paper with more attention than she had given to the rest.

"Wilton has no place of his own; Lawleigh is his uncle's. What of it?"

"There has been a robbery there, and it seems such a curious story altogether. Shall I read it to you?"

He nodded assent, and she read aloud accordingly, a statement, more or less correct, of

the recent scenes at Lawleigh Hall, the seat of
Rupert Clavering, Esq. It struck the three at
once, as being a very singular affair, and the
same idea came into the minds of mother and
daughter at once.

" Mornay ! — was not that the name,
mamma——"

"It was, I am certain." Their heads were
bent together over the paper, which lay on the
table between them.

" There may be many of the same name, of
course, but her husband coming in that strange
way——"

" That is just what I was thinking."

There was a short silence; Herbert, who
had listened attentively, watched them both,
but said nothing. A clatter of little feet at
that moment reminded Clara of her duties;
she turned reluctantly towards the door.

" Those odious brats again!" ejaculated her

brother, in a tone of hasty annoyance; "how I do hate the sound of their tongues, and the sight of their traps all about the place! I wish either they or I were out of it."

Clara's eyes fell on him with an appealing expression that at times had a salutary effect, but this morning only irritated him the more. "I do!" he repeated, "and what is more, ten to one that my wish is fulfilled, Clara, for all your disapproving looks. Mother," as his sister, with a patient sigh, closed the door behind her, "mother, it is of no use to be mysterious. I know what you two have been hinting—you think you have found Mrs. Atterbury."

"It is just possible, Herbert. Poor thing! I have often wished to know what became of her."

"And, of course, you think, too, that this romantic visit was paid her by one you do not like to name. No wonder. But I have

done breakfast, so it will not choke me—
quite."

" I can only conjecture, as you do. I should
think better of him if he has really risked his
own safety to see his wife. But what do you
think yourself?"

" I am afraid it is too good news to be true,
said Herbert, folding up the newspaper. Mrs.
Tresham started a little at the tone of his voice,
and laid her finger on his arm.

" Herbert, remember !"

" No need to tell me that, mother.   No fear
of my forgetting."

" Remember *whose* blessing she shared with
us—*whose* head was resting on her bosom when
he spoke his last words—*who* forgave, and bade
you forgive also, the wrongs he felt for us, not
for himself;—remember all this, and you will
feel as we do, that Eleanor Atterbury is sacred,
and none of us should so much as add a grain

of sand's weight to the heavy burden she has to bear !"

The youth made no answer; he kept his eyes on the table, but showed no symptoms of disrespectful impatience. His lips were closer set than usual, and that was all.

" Are you going out, my dear ?" she asked, presently, seeing him move to the door.

" Yes, mother. I have people to see this morning, and one or two things to do. I may not be in to dinner. By the way, can you let me have another pound or two in advance till my book is sold? I hate having nothing in my pocket."

She shook her head, almost smiling at the manner in which this was said, as if the sensation was peculiar to himself; and taking out her purse, gave him half its scanty contents.

" You must not expect more, dear, for some time. I am obliged to tell you this, as every shilling is calculated upon, and we must not get into debt, you know."

"No, mother, don't. You would never stand it. It takes a great deal of practice to hold up your head like a man, with a hundred pound weight round your neck. I do my best, but it is a failure sometimes. Don't look at me so, though, mother. I can stand anything but that. Good-bye."

"Shall you be out all day? And your writing——?"

"Oh, I do that best when it is all quiet; don't be afraid—it will be all done. I get materials as I go along; geniuses are often hardest at work when they seem most idle, you know." He gave her a hasty kiss, and caught his hat from its peg, without stopping to look if it had been brushed to his mind—a point on which he was usually fastidious.

For some little way he walked on, with long,

eager strides, but his impatience growing too strong, even for his activity, he hailed an omnibus going to the City, and jumped in. The speed of the vehicle was not proportioned to his haste, but in course of time he was deposited in one of the crowded thoroughfares, whence he diverged through sundry smaller streets, till he reached a small dingy eating-house, into which he turned, as if quite familiar with the locality, took his place in one of the boxes, and rapped with a penny on the table for the waiter. A very doubtful-looking individual answered the summons.

" Mr. Lockwood been here to-day?"

" No, sir."

" Run round to the office, and ask him to step here, will you?"

" Yes, sir."

Herbert was sufficiently well known as a liberal customer, to command ready attention to his wishes, and after about twenty minutes' restless expectation, the person he had summoned made his appearance — a quiet, respectable-looking man, whom no one would notice as anything particular, unless they happened to remark how keen his eyes were. He touched his hat to young Tresham, and smiled good-humoured acquiescence when the latter suggested a glass of ale, more as if he knew it would please the young gentleman, than as if he cared for the refreshment itself.

"Well, sir," he said, cheerfully, as they sat together, "how is the world going with you now?   Any better?"

"Badly enough, Lockwood.   I shall come into the force, after all, I expect."

"You think so, sir?   You might do better, and, no doubt, you might do worse.   But it is one thing to go about, and look on, out of curiosity, as a gentleman, and another to do the work. Anything particular to-day?"

" Oh no, nothing of consequence, I dare say. Have you seen the *Times?*" He put the paragraph about Lawleigh before his companion, who read it composedly, and nodded his head. " I had heard all about that," he said; "we have got the man's photograph, and descriptions of the trinkets. We shall have him soon, I dare say, if that is what you want."

" Lockwood, you remember that reward that we talked about some time ago, and which you made sure of winning, but did not?"

" We get thrown out sometimes, sir, certainly," said the other, smiling. " No great blame to us either."

" I think I can show you how to get it now."

" Indeed, sir?"

Herbert leaned across the table, and whis-

pered in his companion's ear. The latter
raised his eyebrows as he listened, and nodded
once or twice encouragingly. "It is worth
trying," he said, after a little thought, "if it
is done at once; but we must take care not
to give any alarm. Are you known down
there?"

"No; I have been asked to go, but never
screwed up my courage. I know I should be
welcome at any time, but——"

"If you know that, sir, it will be very un-
gracious to stay away. Just you do as I bid
you, and we'll touch the money yet, if it is to
be had in that quarter."

"It is not for the money, Lockwood, I do it,
though I want it badly enough. That man,
or his father, or both, caused my father's death
as much as if they had shot him, and I'd drag
the fellow out of Windsor Castle, sooner than
let him escape again."

"Quite right, sir; but if you mean to do the job, you must keep cool, and obey orders. Otherwise, I can do nothing. Do you understand ?"

Herbert bit his lip, but assented, and the rest of the conversation passed with their heads so close to each other, it would have been impossible for the keenest listener to overhear what was said.

When they separated, Tresham got into a cab ; a shilling or two seemed of little consequence at such a time—and went full speed to the lodgings of Charles Lyle. The curate was fortunately at home, taking his somewhat uncomfortable meal, with a book open by his plate, and a pile of papers under his hat at the other end of his table. He started up on Tresham's entrance, nearly sending the whole of his dinner equipage on to the floor.

"Herbert, old fellow! How are you?

Nothing the matter, is there ? No ? All right, then. Sit down, if you can find a chair. Here, we'll soon clear this," tilting the one most readily got hold of, so that the heap of odds and ends tumbled promiscuously upon the rug; "bring yourself to an anchor there for a minute, and have a chop—will you ?"

The hospitality of the offer was not so apparent as it deserved; for the said chop, uninviting as it might be, was his only chance of dinner for that day, and Charles Lyle had been racing about his parish, or exerting his lungs in his particularly noisy schools, the whole morning. Herbert declined hastily, with a hint at a late breakfast.

" Ah, you were at work all night, I suppose. That is not the best thing in the world for you, is it ?"

" It cannot be helped, Lyle, in these times, you know. The publishers will pay for all that, by-and-bye. I wanted to talk to you for a minute."

" Excuse my going on with my dinner, then, for I have an appointment in half an hour. Anything I can do ?"

" Well, yes,—if not inconvenient—could you lend me a five-pound note ? You shall have it again in a few days."

" I hope so, for it is the only one I have, and you know my dread of *tick*. Find it, my boy," throwing him his porte-monnaie, " only leave me the silver, or I shall have to come on the parish for a loaf. I am sorry you are so hard up. Tell Clara I have the promise of two fresh pupils for her. I have no time to write to-day. Are you going so soon ?"

" Yes, thank you, my dear fellow. I have business to do. Much obliged for this," taking the solitary note out of the purse; " I would not ask you if it were not an urgent case. Go and see them to-morrow, if you possibly can. And if they are down-hearted about me, tell them I am sure to succeed, there's a good fellow."

" I will, if you will set my mind at ease on one point.   You are not going to do anything with that money that your mother would not approve ?"

The youth grew scarlet, and clenched it in his hand.

" Charles, I cannot stand lecturing, you know that; and I won't be suspected.   If you doubt me, take your money back again."

"That is hardly gracious, Herbert: you know if there were a dozen more where that came from, you would be welcome to them all. Only it goes to my heart to see your dear mother look so careworn."

" Do you think, then, it does not go to *mine ?* I do believe you all consider me next to a brute, without feeling for a soul but myself. Don't ask me any more questions, Lyle ; I am only doing what I have a right—what my father's son ought to do—but I must not speak of it beforehand. Good-bye. You will know all in time." And he hurried away, threw himself into his cab, and drove home.

Mrs. Tresham was surprised, and rather vexed, when her son, bidding the Hansom wait, ran hastily into her little parlour, where she sat at work, to announce that he was going out of town for a day or two, on private business. She had never compelled him to tell her more of his proceedings than he chose, but this seemed such an unnecessary expense at that moment, that she could not but remonstrate, and entreat for some explanation. He kissed her affectionately, returning part of the money she had given him in the morning, threw out hints about a scheme, and a sharp friend, and promises of secresy, and contrived to restore her spirits to a more confident state. Anxious to avoid the cross-questioning of his sisters, he was very expeditious over his carpet-bag, and was gone before his mother recollected that he had given her no address, nor even said when he should return.

That night he and his friend Lockwood slept at the Lion Inn, Hadlow.

"We must take care what we are about, sir," was the whispered greeting Herbert received in the morning, when he met his confederate alone. "There is another party here on the same errand, if I am not very much mistaken, which, I may say, is not often."

"One of your people?"

"Not exactly, sir. He is too old for one of us; more like a lawyer, to my thinking. He has just ordered his breakfast. If you step this way, you will see him."

Tresham obeyed, and looking through the window of the bar into the public room, at once recognised the person in question.

"You know him, sir?" whispered Lockwood, as the young man stepped back.

"Yes. He was Atterbury's solicitor."

"That looks like business. Is he here for or against them, do you think?"

"Against."

"Then we must decide either to take him into our counsel, or to get the start of him— that is, supposing he is here on our errand. Will he know you?"

"I dare say he will."

"Then you must breakfast here, out of his way. I'll arrange all that with the landlady. I have had a talk with her already. I shall go and have a cup of coffee along with the gentleman, and see what I can make of him."

Herbert ate his breakfast, and waited impatiently for his ally. The latter came back to him at last, as cool and good tempered as ever, even when reproached with being so slow.

" He is after something, sir, that is certain, but he is one of your close ones. They are always a trouble at first. Now, the thing to be ascertained is, if the party we want is at the Hall or not; if he is not, and this one is in his secret, he will go to the place where he is to be found; but if this one is no wiser than ourselves, he will, most likely, go straight up to the Hall, as we should do. You see, we may be on the wrong trail after all, and if ever you mean to be one of us, Mr. Tresham, you must practise patience, which, it strikes me, you forgot to put up in your carpet-bag yesterday."

Herbert shrugged his shoulders; but he took a rebuke from the friend of his own making better than from those whom he was expected to attend to, and professed himself as docile and cool as possible. It was, therefore, soon arranged, that he should walk leisurely, as if for his private enjoyment, to pay his call at Lawleigh, leaving his confederate to keep watch over the proceedings of Mr. Martock.

"You'll do nothing, of course, without consulting me, Lockwood?"

"Of course not, sir; you are to get me all the information, you know. This is your job, and you will have all the credit."

"Credit? I doubt its reflecting much of that on either of us. Do you know, Lockwood, I have half a mind to let it alone."

"Oh no, you have not, sir; quite the contrary. You are going to carry it through with the same spirit and intelligence with which you began, and here is your hat, sir, nicely brushed, and you'll go and call on your friends as if you had nothing in the world on your mind, and a great deal in your pocket. You understand."

He made no reply, but set out as desired. Just as he had passed the vicarage gate, he met Edward Wilton, with an elderly gentleman, whom he supposed must be his uncle, and a very ungainly specimen of an uncle too.

" Why, Tresham, who would have thought of seeing you here? Have you changed your mind, and are you come to be introduced to my uncle, after all?"

" I hope to have that pleasure, certainly," said Herbert, glancing at the elderly gentleman as he spoke, " but I am not come to intrude upon him or you. I had business in the neighbourhood, so I thought I could not be so near without calling at Lawleigh."

"I should think not. Will you go and call there now? I wish I could go back with you, but I have business, too, this morning, and must keep my appointment. Mr. Shannon— allow me to introduce Mr. Herbert Tresham." The gentlemen looked sharply at each other, and exchanged bows. "If you will walk on, Tresham, and send in your name, you will find Mrs. Sydney and Miss Clavering at home, and I will follow as soon as I can. That is your nearest way—across that field, through the plantation."

Tresham followed his instructions, and reached the Hall without any greater adventure than meeting a policeman, lounging about —a sight that had been by no means uncommon of late. He stopped to ask his way, not because he could not find it, but in hopes of extracting something from the functionary. He learned that people were always coming down to look at the place, and they were driven wild with questions about the secret closet.

"Is the gentleman who was shut up in it still there, do you know?"

"I believe he is, sir.   He was badly hurt, they say."

" A singular circumstance, is it not, that such a thing should exist, and be forgotten by the family?"

"Well, sir, it is, rather; but I heard Mr. Clavering explain how that was.   It seems there was an accident happened when his grandfather was a boy; a little brother of his was shut up in it by a playfellow, out of mischief, and was taken out an idiot for life; and after that, the closet was never opened, and never talked about, so it came to be almost forgotten, as you say."

"Ah, thank you—very interesting indeed,"

said Herbert; and he walked on, unconscious
that he had set the policeman conjecturing,
and that the latter watched him till he was out
of sight.

The ladies received him with all the cordial
kindness Edward had promised, though he
could see it was a relief when he explained he
was not come to stay. He was so much
charmed with Miss Clavering's personal at-
tractions, and agreeable conversation, that he
almost forgot his purpose for a time, and gave
himself up to the enjoyment of the hour. Mr.
Clavering was out on business, but he was
invited to luncheon, when he would meet him,
and willingly agreed to remain. Gradually it
dawned on him that time was getting on, and
he had learned nothing. He led the conversation to the robbery. Miss Clavering was evidently prepared for this, and answered some of
his questions readily, though briefly, while she

quietly turned others aside.   No hints that he could throw out led to any discovery, nor did she appear to have anything particular to conceal.   It was nearly one o'clock, and he was wondering what he should do next, when a card was brought in by Adam's successor, with the explanation that it was "for Mrs. Mornay."

"Did you say Mrs. Mornay was too unwell to receive visitors?"

"Yes, ma'am, but the gentleman said he had come on business, and he asked if Mr. Shannon was here, and said he would wait to see him, if not inconvenient."

"Ask him into the drawing-room," said Anne, signifying by that name a small but cheerful apartment lately rescued from obscurity, and which they were furnishing by degrees.   Herbert waited till the servant had withdrawn, and then came up to Miss Clavering, as she stood in silent thought, with a smile full of meaning and intelligence.

"Shall I not then have the pleasure of seeing Mrs. Mornay to-day?"

"Mrs. Mornay? Do you know her, then?"

"I believe I do; if she is the lady I mean, certainly; and I do not think I am mistaken."

"Did you say you wished to see her?"

"Not if she is too unwell, and I am not even sure that I am correct. Perhaps you would be good enough to let her have my card, and if she owns my acquaintance, would kindly tell her how sorry I am to have so poor an account to take of her to my mother."

His manner was so confident, Anne could not doubt he was in the secret, and, to satisfy her mind, went away directly. In about a quarter of an hour she returned, looking rather agitated.

"Mr. Tresham, I am afraid I have done

very wrong, but my friend begs to see you for a few minutes, and I dare not refuse her. Will you mind coming up-stairs with me? I need not ask you to be cautious not to excite her by too much conversation, as she has been ordered quietness, and talking brings back her cough."

Young Tresham had not expected this; he had taken it for granted that if it was Eleanor, she would avoid seeing him; but he could find no excuse for refusal, and followed Miss Clavering, without having the least made up his mind what he should say or do.

Ever since Eleanor's attack, Anne had given her up her room, as being larger than her own, and having a small dressing-room opening into it. In this dressing-room Herbert found Mrs. Atterbury, sadly changed since he saw her last, reclining on pillows in an easy-chair—her delicate features wasted and colourless, except a hectic spot on each cheek, and her eyes looking unusually large, with the patient languor of weakness and suffering in them, which was now becoming habitual. She sat up with an effort, as the youth approached, and held out a hand, so thin and transparent, he hardly ventured to take it in his strong fingers. The touch gave him a strange thrill; he began to wish his scheme abandoned, or that it had never been begun.

"How did you find me out?" was her first question, asked with no little anxiety.

He murmured something about the *Times*.

"You remember, Mrs. Atterbury, my mother knew you went by the name of Mornay. She has tried very often to obtain news of you."

"She is very good; I have often thought of her kindness—of your sisters'. Indeed I have. Will you sit down close to me, and then I need not speak loud."

He complied; his heart failing him more and more.

"I had not courage to see them again—I should not have seen you now, only I may never have another opportunity, and I have something to tell you. I know something of your trials—forgive my naming them"—she put her hand on Herbert's arm as she spoke; "if I had not suffered too, I should not dare to do so. May I go on?" for his downcast, gloomy looks gave her little encouragement.

"It is not of much use, Mrs. Atterbury," he muttered, clenching his hand on his knee; "we must bear them, whatever they are."

"Can you forgive them too?"

"Oh, of course, of course," and he looked at her with a smile, that made her shiver, her hands dropping on her knees. There was a short silence before she said, in a feeble voice,

"I understood that Clara—that you wished for an Indian chaplaincy for Mr. Lyle?"

"To be sure; he has a wretched curacy that works him to death. He would be glad of anything, but we are not likely to get it."

"I have tried—I tell you, in case of anything happening—I wrote to my cousin, Mr. Ormonde, who fills a high position in India, and has great interest, and begged him, as the only favour I should ask, that he would do what he could for your mother's school, and get Mr. Lyle made a chaplain. I hope I shall have an answer by the return mail. One thing more," stopping his stammered attempt at thanks; "most fortunately, just before this robbery, I had given most of my jewels to Mr. Wilton to dispose of for me, and had not received the proceeds. I had reserved them, that if any pressing claim came to my knowledge, I might have some means of meeting it,

however small." She took his hand, and he
felt a small packet glide into it. "I have no
right," she added, hurriedly, "I should not
presume to make presents ; I only wish to pay
a very, very small part of a debt I feel heavily
enough, believe me. I wish I could do more,
but if you would accept this, it might enable
you to buy books, or, by relieving your mind
of some of your anxiety, enable you to work
better—or, perhaps——"

Her breath failed her here, and she sank
back on her pillows, while he sat with his
head down, holding the packet between his
fingers, and struggling with the contending
passions that she had unconsciously stirred up.
Money? he wanted every farthing as if it were
vital air; his mother's exhausted purse —
Charles Lyle's porte-monnaie—those dunning
letters in his pocket—he had them all before
his eyes—and had he not a right to take what

was acknowledged to be only his due? But then, if he took her money, could he betray her husband? and if he spared him, should he not feel he had made a merchandise of his revenge?

Again and again, as he sat there, thinking, he wished he had never come.

She watched him with increasing fear; and when he raised his eyes, he was rather dismayed to see how faint she looked. She signed to him to give her some lemonade that was on the table, and he supported her while she drank. She smiled as she thanked him.

" I have not offended you?"

" Whom *could* you offend, Mrs. Atterbury?"

" Then let me see you put that in your pocket, and I shall feel sure that there is no quarrel between us."

" You know we have no quarrel with *you*,"

he said, with emphasis. " It has been a cruel shame all along, that you have been exposed to bear the brunt of all this. None but the worst of cowards would have done it. Yes," raising his voice, in spite of her imploring gesture, " the worst of cowards — who can shelter himself from the resentment of those he has injured, behind the helplessness and generosity of his innocent wife. If he were a man worthy the name, he would come forward, and face the worst, and take the penalty; and not all my sense of what is due to your merit and misfortunes, would prevent me—*ought* to prevent me, if I have the power——"

" From what? Herbert Tresham, from what?" she repeated, holding him fast with both her feeble hands: "do you forget the last scene we shared together—the pardon, the blessing given to us both, and won on my knees, by my tears, for *him?* Do you forget what he said to you, just as his head fell back on my shoulder?—was his pardon nothing—the pardon of a dying saint, given when his heart was breaking? Must I kneel to you to renew it? I would, indeed I would—but I am so weak, so broken with all this——"

Her strength was exhausted, and the cough returning with fearful vehemence, she put her handkerchief quickly to her mouth. Tresham was horrified by the sight of blood; he called loudly for help, so loudly, that the door of the bedroom was hastily opened, and Atterbury rushed in. Without noticing Herbert, he devoted himself to the sufferer, attending upon her with an assiduous care and readiness that showed he was accustomed to the office, and by his gentle, but decided manner of speaking, helping her to command herself sooner than she could have done alone. When she was once more comparatively at ease, he turned, for the first time, to look at his old friend's son.

"I do not blame you, Tresham, for what you said. It is all too just, and it comes from *you*. But you might have spared *her*, knowing what she is."

"*You* have not spared her, Mr. Atterbury," said Herbert, sternly.

"It is very true, I have not," and Frederick bent over his wife, and smoothed the damp hair that had fallen on her pillow, "but I would, if I knew how."

Herbert stood watching him in silence. It was difficult to realise that that sunburnt, shabbily-dressed man, whose manner betrayed such deep humiliation, could be the young and brilliant model that had dazzled him two years ago, and of whose patronising notice he had then felt so proud.

"I do not want to hurt Mrs. Atterbury's

feelings," he said at last. " I am very sorry
for her, as she must know. But I have others
at home who have gone through as much"—
he set his teeth with suppressed passion—" and
I am nearly torn to pieces with fellows bullying
me for money besides—not that I mean to take
this," flinging the packet on the table, "but it
is quite enough to drive a man to do hard
things, you know——"

" What things ?" said Atterbury, looking
quickly round. Eleanor caught the alarm in
his look and tone, and made a desperate effort
to speak—to plead—to do something, she knew
not what, but her head only dropped on her
husband's shoulder, and he, with an impe-
rative gesture to Tresham to be silent, lifted
her as if she had been an infant, and carried
her to the bed in the next room. It was some
little while before he could venture to leave
her, and when, on her sinking into a kind of

languid torpor, he returned to the dressing-room, to learn the worst, Herbert Tresham was gone—not only from that apartment, but from the house.

" It is of no use, Mr. Shannon. No denial or equivocation will have the slightest effect on me. I know he is here."

" You always know more than other people, Mr. Martock: more than actually happens, sometimes. You knew, for instance, that Mrs. Atterbury did not wish to have any communication with me, except through you—an arrangement which led to my not communicating with her at all, as you probably foresaw; and which she has denied, point blank !"

" Mrs. Atterbury's denials are irrelevant at present. I speak plainly, and I will be answered plainly. I have had my eye on both a long while, and I know they are both here now. You know, too, that every hour that young man is in England, is spent in jeopardy. In another four-and-twenty hours nothing can save him. He has no means of procuring bail, if it would be accepted; he will be in prison for months, most likely for years."

"Pleasant news, if true. But why you take the trouble of telling it, I don't see."

"You will see plainly enough, before I have done. Mrs. Atterbury deceived me once; she entered into an arrangement by which my claims would have been partially satisfied, and afterwards broke it off. Those claims remain, and unless attended to, her husband is lost. Make her understand that, if you please."

"How do you expect a poor woman to satisfy anybody's claim, when she has given up everything she has in the world?"

"She has a rich and liberal relation in India."

"I know; Mr. Ormonde. He will not be applied to, if you mean that."

" He has been applied to."

" He has? By whom?"

" By myself."

" Upon my honour, Mr. Martock—you are the most——"

" Suppose we defer epithets and comments, Mr. Shannon, till the more important part of our business is over."

" Very well; but I warn you, Mr. Martock, if they go on accumulating too long, the interest will amount to something serious."

"I wrote to Mr. Ormonde," continued the other, without choosing to notice this remark, " telling him of the deplorable condition in which his cousin was left, and the disgrace to which the family name might be exposed, if none of her relations came forward to shield it by liberal sacrifices. And this is his answer."

He gave the letter to Mr. Shannon. It was a short, courteous reply, guardedly worded, as if the writer felt too much, and trusted too little, to dare give vent; and purporting, that if Mrs. Frederick Atterbury would herself communicate with him, and plainly state her wishes, and the sum she required, he would do his best to serve her, for her father's sake. He had already given orders to his agents to honour her draft for a handsome amount, which was stated.

"Nothing can be more gentlemanly, certainly," was Mr. Shannon's comment. "I may give this to her, of course."

"Of course. And you will represent to her, that her husband's fate is now in her hands. If she will pledge her word that she will obtain from Mr. Ormonde what I require, or even a considerable part of it—I will pledge mine that Frederick Atterbury is allowed to leave the kingdom unmolested—a pledge no one can give but myself.   Do not let her flatter herself a trial will be a light matter.   It will be terrible—and he knows it—even though he may not quite know why."

"Well, it may be so; but if I were Mr. Atterbury, I should be inclined to face it, notwithstanding."

"You would?   After what I have said?"

"The rather that you *have* said it."

"Then my suspicion was correct.   You have those papers."

Before any answer could be returned to this, there fell on their ears a sound that made them both start up, look at each other, and, by a common impulse, rush to the door, and stand listening, in alarm and consternation.

Mr. Clavering and Edward were just wondering at young Tresham's strange behaviour in slipping out of the house without waiting to see them, and were debating whether to go after him or not, when they were told a person had called to speak to the gentlemen and ladies about the robbery. As this might, or might not be a true story, Wilton went to reconnoitre, and found an old man, calling himself a jeweller, but looking more like a Jew pawnbroker than anything else, who announced that an article had been offered him for sale, which he thought must have been stolen, and had therefore detained—that, on inquiry, it seemed probable it might be one of those lately lost, and he had come to see if the lady who was robbed would identify it. On being asked to produce the article, he demurred; he would rather show it to the lady herself; as if she could describe it first, it would be more satisfactory. The lady was too unwell, Wilton told him, to be disturbed just

then, and he went to consult his uncle and
cousin.   The old man had suggested that the
lady's husband might do as well, and the
question was, could Atterbury run the risk?
Mr. Clavering went to his room, to ask what
he would do.   He found him in the dressing-
room, surrounded with papers and accounts,
but evidently much too miserable to do anything to any purpose.   Eleanor had fallen
asleep, and must not be disturbed.   He would
come and look at the trinket; he should know
it, if it were really hers.   So the Jew was
shown into Anne's little room, where Anne
and the three gentlemen were waiting to receive him.   Atterbury described his wife's
watch and chain, and the little trinkets and
rings that had been taken, but the Jew shook
his head.   It was neither of those; he would
show it to the gentleman; if he could swear to
it, that would be sufficient.   And he pulled out

a box, in which was a gold bracelet. Was that the thing?

"Yes," said Atterbury, not daring to lift his eyes. "I can swear to it."

"So can I," said Miss Clavering; "I remember it perfectly." The calmness of her voice was some relief; he blessed her for it in his heart.

"Is there anything by which you can identify it?" asked Mr. Clavering.

The Jew looked from one to the other. They exchanged a glance—how much it said no one could tell but themselves—and then Atterbury observed, that there was a secret spring in the clasp.

"And the clasp contains a picture," added Anne. She looked at her cousin now, and meeting his eyes bent on her, full of serious, earnest inquiry, returned such an answer as he who knew her so well could alone understand and appreciate. If he had doubted of her self-conquest before, the frank contrition of that look must have convinced him.

" Do you wish the clasp to be opened ?" asked Rupert of the Jew. He owned it would be satisfactory; it was unfastened accordingly, and the picture recognised by all, for the likeness so skilfully painted, defied the changes of time.   The evidence was all the Jew desired; he described the party who had tried to sell it to him, a description answering in all respects to that of Adam, and dwelt on his own acuteness in having at once detected his dishonesty, and compelled him to leave it by threats of the police. Before giving up the trinket to the owner, he only begged leave to speak to him alone for two minutes. The others accordingly withdrew, and Atterbury, concluding the reward was in question, was beginning to assure him it was all safe, when the old man stopped him short.

" Don't you be uneasy, sir; I don't want

your money at all. I am only come because it
is my duty, and I am sure you will own I have
done it civilly. I wish to be civil, and unless
you give me reason, I shall not behave otherwise, but"—and he pulled off his white hair
and his infirmities in the same moment, and his
voice became decided and peremptory—"my
name is Lockwood, of the detective police, and
Mr. Atterbury, you are my prisoner."

For one bitter moment—only one—the heart
of the unfortunate young man swelled as if it
would burst; and that moment was of no small
peril to his captor and himself; but the next,
he had recovered his calmness, and Lockwood's
practised eye saw there was nothing more to
fear.

"I will go with you quietly, I give you my
word," said Atterbury; "but tell me one thing
first—how did you find out I was here?"

"Well, sir, I have been on the look-out for

you a long time, but I must frankly confess I was put on the scent by a young gentleman, though he was too young to be trusted to carry the matter through."

" You don't mean it was Tresham's doing ? What am I saying ? It is retribution—and it is just. You will let me consult my friends ?"

"Certainly, sir; only I must keep you in sight. That is my duty."

Frederick opened the door, and the paleness of his face told them the truth, even before they saw the transformation of the supposed jeweller. Mr. Clavering, indignant at such a proceeding under his roof, was beginning to expostulate fiercely, but Atterbury begged him to forbear.

" It is only just—it must have come sooner or later. Thank you for all your kindness to me. I beg your pardon for exposing Miss Clavering to such a scene."

" Oh, do not think of me!" said Anne—
" your wife, Mr. Atterbury—how shall we tell
her this?"

His lips worked convulsively. " I must see
her for a minute. Officer, will you trust me?
You can stand outside; but she must not see
you, or it may be her death."

" I will trust you, sir, though I must stand at
the door. It is only my duty that obliges me
to do it, and if you deal like a gentleman with
me, I will treat you as one."

" Thank you. Does any one know where
Mr. Shannon is?"

He was coming towards him at that moment, and behind him appeared a face that
Frederick little expected to see; and at whose
aspect he flushed so furiously, that Lockwood
came a step nearer.

" *You* here, too? This is *your* doing, is
it?"

" No, upon my honour," said Mr. Martock, earnestly; " ask the officer—ask Mr. Shannon —I had nothing whatever to do with it. On the contrary, I came to try and save you. I can save you still. Listen," drawing him aside, " I will get bail for you—I will pull you through altogether, if your wife agrees to my terms, and everything is put into my hands. Say the word, and we are friends again—to-morrow it will be too late !"

" Mr. Shannon, please to step here," said Frederick. " This gentleman has been proposing terms—do you recommend my taking them ?"

" That depends, Mr. Atterbury, on the opinion you may have of him who offers them. I have my own—but that is of less consequence."

" If that be all, it is soon decided. Hear me, sir, for the last time—for I imagine you

will hardly repeat these offers of friendship—
when I was in this house before, I was comparatively an innocent man—my name was
not dishonoured—my conscience had not the
sufferings of others to bear. I go out of it to-
day to prison—indebted to the goodness of
those I have wronged for kindnesses I can
never repay—and before them, I say to you,
evil genius that you have been to my father
and myself—I would rather die in that prison,
than escape it through your advice and help;
for never yet did any one accept a service from
you, that was not paid for by some innocent
person's misery. What the hold was you had
on him that is gone, is best known to yourself
—I know what it brought him to, and never,
if I can help it, shall you use such a power
again. Mr. Shannon—Mr. Clavering—I have
spoken freely before you, that you may do me
the service, if necessary, of repeating to my

wife what has passed; and of impressing on her mind my solemn injunction to have nothing to do with this gentleman whatever, let him threaten or promise what he will. Now, Mr. Lockwood, as I see you are growing impatient, if you will allow me, I will get ready to go with you."

There was a dead silence. The officer made a civil inclination of the head, and followed him up-stairs. Mr. Martock, whose face had grown the colour of lead, took up his hat, and smoothing it mechanically with his sleeve, moved to the door. No one attempted to stop him. Mr. Clavering's courtesy induced him to make a stiff bow, which was barely returned, and all seemed to feel a weight off their minds when he was safely out of the house.

By this time, Mrs. Sydney and Arthur had learned what had happened, and the one feel-

ing uppermost in all their minds, was first expressed by the kind old lady, "How will that
poor wife of his get over it?" The rush of tears
that came to Anne Clavering's eyes—unselfish
tears, for others, not herself—were very beau-
tiful in those of Edward Wilton. He took her
aside while Uncle Rupert was consulting with
Mr. Shannon, and whispered a suggestion that
brought a gleam of loving gratitude to her
face. "Uncle Rupert is right—there are not
two men like you in the world, Edward," was
all her answer, but there was quite enough in
the look and tone to make his heart bound in a
manner that, at such a moment, almost seemed
inhuman.

Atterbury's preparations did not take long;
he had too few things with him to give much
trouble, and the courtesy of his captor was not
over-taxed. The trial came when all was
ready, and he had to pay his last visit to his

wife.   He trembled like a child as he opened
the door, and the officer's pity was so far
moved, that he whispered to him not to lose
heart; if the magistrates would take bail, he
would see her again before long.

"Tell her, you are obliged to go up about
the robbery, and if you seem to take it quietly,
she will suspect nothing."

He made no answer, but signed to him to
close the door, and went softly up to her bedside.   She lay in the attitude in which he had
left her, sleeping so tranquilly, he stood hesi-
tating what to do.   To wake her seemed so
cruel—but to leave her without one kiss, would
be more cruel still.   She spared him the choice
by opening her eyes, and, smiling to see him
bending over her, put up her hand to draw
him gently down, till his face was close to
hers.   He could not have spoken calmly at
that moment, but he folded her in a long,

fervent embrace, in which all the deep remorse of his soul would fain have poured itself forth; and then as silently released himself from her hold, and tried to leave her. Her eyes were on him, and quickened by the daily fear in which she had been living, she read that in his that made her raise herself with a start.

" Frederick !"

The piteous cry stopped him when he had almost reached the door; his fortitude was nearly unmanned; he stepped hastily back to the bedside, and, kneeling beside it, clasped her in his arms again.

" Eleanor, my love—my own—I must leave you for a little while—only a little while, I hope," he faltered, feeling her arms cling round his neck as if death only should divide them. "You will help me to bear this parting, will you not? You will be my support, as you have been before, by praying for me—you will bear up for my sake, that I may find you better when I come back, will you not?" he whispered again and again, terrified by her silence, and the strength of that nervous clasp of the wasted arms. But their hold relaxed even as he was speaking, and the lips and brow he kissed so despairingly, seemed growing cold beneath his touch. He sprang to his feet, almost beside himself with agony, and hardly knowing what he did, might have driven Lockwood to use severe measures, had not Anne Clavering been on the watch, and hurried in at his cry for help. She drew him gently from the bed, and took his place by Eleanor's pillow. "Leave your wife to me, Mr. Atterbury," she said, holding out her disengaged hand, the tears running down her cheeks the while, "trust her to me—I will guard her night and day, and comfort her if I can; and my cousin is going up with you to London, and will not leave you while you want a friend."

"God reward you," was all he could reply,

but he pressed his lips on her hand, and left it moistened with his tears; and that moment, sorrowful as it was, and realising, as it did, the unalterable fact, that a gulf lay between them for ever, which they would not now pass if they could, was the first in which the one felt he was forgiven, and the other that she had nothing to forgive.

CHAPTER IV.

VELLONI'S.

IT was the evening of a sultry July day in Brussels, in which everybody had been expecting and longing for thunder and lightning, on the principle that when things come to the worst, they mend,—that the desire for something like air and refreshment drove a crowd of residents and visitors to their favourite *café* in the Park, where, seated under the trees, with the help of an excellent band, and a liberal allowance of ices and coffee, they might hope, for a little while, to forget the glare and suffocation of the last hours. Several English parties were there, on their way to other parts of the Continent; and among these a group with which our readers are familiar; consisting of Mrs. Cummings and Sophia, Mr. and Mrs. Prynne, and the Messrs. Blatherwick. The Prynnes had joined the party only a day or two before, having spent the spring and early summer in travelling; and it was still undecided where they should all go next—a fortunate circumstance for a gentleman of his temperament, as it admitted of endless debate and a great deal of quarrelling.

"Perfectly atrocious to think of stopping *here !*" pronounced Mr. Prynne, as, after swallowing three ices and two glasses of liqueur, he threw himself back on his chair, and gave vent to his feelings in sublime disregard of the touching sounds the first violin was drawing out at the moment. "The most odious place I ever saw in my life! France without its vivacity—Germany without its taste—England without its comfort; nothing but dust and sand and glare; not a picture, not a church worth looking at; and bores from sweet home coming up to shake hands with you at the corner of every street! I vote we start to-morrow."

Now Mr. Blatherwick senior had, perhaps, grumbled at the heat, and the fatigue of a long walk up and down the picturesque old streets, as heartily as any Briton in the whole place; but Mr. Prynne's sweeping abuse called up his love of fair play, especially as he noticed that some of the guests within hearing were listening with strong expressions of disgust. "If people never choose to be pleased abroad, they had better go home, that is what I think. I never expected, for my part, to be without hot weather in July, and certainly, it is pleasant enough, sitting out here, if one was allowed to hear the music in peace. You would not go away without seeing Waterloo, would you, sir?"

"I wouldn't get out of this chair to see Waterloo. I consider the old Duke was a very overrated man."

"Indeed. Well, that alters the case."

"Decidedly overrated. The fact is, the press made him what he was; everybody puffed him up, and then everybody believed it, till he believed it himself. It is pretty well acknowledged now, that the Peninsular war was a blunder from beginning to end, and that Spain would much rather have kept Joseph, and would have been much better off."

"What a pity you were not in office in those days, Mr. Prynne. To be sure, we should not be enjoying your conversation now, in all probability, but for the good of unborn generations we might put up with that. Indeed, it strikes me that some of our neighbours would be happy to dispense with it as it is."

"There, do be quiet, dear," said the bride, impatiently. "I want to hear this player of all things, and you are making everybody stare by talking so loud."

A chorus of "Hush!" in various languages, and several emphatic gestures of discontent, silenced Mr. Prynne for about two minutes and a half, when he began again as if it had been only a gratifying encore.

"Not a performer worth listening to. The worst wind instruments I ever heard; and as for that violin, Wilkie's blind fiddler was a Paganini compared with him. Your Belgians have not an idea about music; and as for painting, I would not trust a sign-post with them!"

"I say, you will have a lantern rigged up for your special benefit, if you go on much longer," said a voice behind him, as a slender, well-dressed figure emerged into the light, and, lifting up his hat to the company, revealed the welcome features of young Compton. "Do you know, Mrs. Cummings," shaking her eagerly-offered hand, "I had only just come in when I heard Prynne's voice, and most of his lecture; and so did three tight-waisted fellows with moustaches as long as my arm, who are all very anxious to learn his name and address."

"Oh, don't say so, Mr. Compton," said Mrs. Cummings; "it would be too dreadful to think about, only I know it is all your fun. Come and sit down and be scolded, for I am very angry with you, and do not mean, indeed, to speak to you at all."

"What shall I do to show my penitence?

I am exceedingly sorry, and won't do it again, especially as I don't know what it is. May I have some ice to keep me in spirits for my punishment? Miss Cummings, you must taste their *plombière;* it is as good as the music, and you are a judge of both. How long have you been in Brussels?"

"Only a day and a half. When did you come?"

"This morning. I have been half over Europe since that delightful evening when I last saw you."

"What gave you such a rage for furious travelling all of a sudden?"

"Did you ever read any of those books, where people go to look for other people, and hunt out their trail, and lose it, and lose themselves, and come back on their tracks, and nose out their way again, till all of a sudden, at the end, we will say, of the third volume, they pounce on the man they want? That is just what I have been doing the last four months."

"And have you succeeded?" asked Sophia, as usual, not half understanding him, but thinking all he said must be clever.

"Well, I have had a long run, but I am in hopes I have come up with him now. I did not expect to find *you* here."

"So, Mr. Compton!" here broke in Mr. Blatherwick, leaning across the little table that his voice might not disturb the company, "you are a close hand at a secret, I find. You knew that poor Mrs. Atterbury was at the Grove, and never told any one."

"How could I, sir, when I had promised I would not?"

"Ah, I am very angry with you, all the same," said Mrs. Cummings, shaking her head, but not implacably. "You are a sad impostor, to say the least of it; and I never mean to believe you again, if you say your leg is broken.",

"Upon my honour I had the toothache—I had indeed; only I thought it a pity it should be wasted, that was all. I wished with all my heart I might have told you the whole truth, Mrs. Cummings, for I know you would have felt for a poor lady in such circumstances."

"You only do me justice. I certainly should. Not but what I did show her every real kindness, and was her friend when she seemed to have no other. I can truly say I bear her and her wretched husband no ill will, and when he has suffered the penalty of his crimes, no one will ever hear me do otherwise than wish he may repent and amend."

"His crimes? that is pretty strong, is it not?"

"I call robbery a crime, my dear Mr. Compton."

"Well, I am so used to be robbed, I have grown to think of it as an amiable weakness. Can they prove he was a robber?"

"I hope so, I am sure."

"I hope not," said Mr. Blatherwick. "Things are turning out as I said they would. I am sorry for his wife, but, for his own sake, I am glad he is taken, for I hope it will show that he was not so guilty as people think."

"I have missed some of the papers," said Compton, "and I do not know all that has passed. How was he caught?"

"Did not you read the wonderful story about his being hid in a secret closet at the Claverings', and his wife being nearly taken up on suspicion of being connected with burglars?"

"I did see that. What idiots people must be! And I heard, too, of a robbery afterwards."

"Well," said Mr. Prynne, disturbed at having been so long left out of the conversation, "didn't you hear that a rich old parson, whom he had fleeced, came down to see the house, and got into his room on pretence of paying him a visit of consolation, and gave notice to the police, and had him taken up there and then? I only hope the old fellow will be made a bishop."

"As usual, sir, your accuracy is of a piece with your good taste and information," observed Mr. Blatherwick, "for I happen to know the party. It was not a clergyman, but his son."

"It is all the same—the old gentleman put him up to it."

"Scarcely. He died two years before."

" He had something to do with it, then. I will bet you a bottle of Sillery he had."

" You are safe enough there, Mr. Prynne. The family were ruined by the failure, and the young man, soured by misfortune, as soon as he suspected Atterbury was the person named in the paper, went down with a detective to arrest him."

" Well, well, it comes to the same thing."

" Not quite, for his mother told me he had never got over it. He was so touched by Mrs. Atterbury's distress, that he tried to undo what he had done, and throw the detective off the scent. But, as you may suppose, the officer was too clever for him, and while Tresham was waiting quietly at the inn, in the belief that he had sent his friend on a wild-goose chase, got into the house in disguise, and was half way to London with his prisoner, before his confederate knew what had passed.

The poor boy went home in a state of distrac-
tion, that nearly threw him into a fever; and
his mother has been anxious about him ever
since."

"I wish I had known all this sooner," said
Compton, musingly. "I have been moving
about so much, no one knew where to write
to me, I suppose. If I had had the least idea
——Ah! there he is at last!"

"Who, Mr. Compton?" asked Sophia, rather
vexed to see him rise to leave their party.

"My friend—so to speak—whom I have
been hunting for. I thought I should meet
him here. Excuse me for ten minutes, and
pay particular attention to the next piece.
They say it is played better here than in any
town in Europe."

He was moving as he said the words, and
walking leisurely up to a table, already occupied by a tall, thin man with a blue shade

over his eyes, took possession of the opposite chair, observing, " So I have found you at last, Despard."

The person thus addressed lifted his head at the sound of his voice, looked at him a few moments without reply, and then stretched out his hand. " Well, Tommy, I did not expect this pleasure, but since you say you have found me, I suppose you have thought me worth looking for, and that is something in these hard times."

" I have been looking for you the last four months."

" I wish I had known it. There has never been a day in the last eight, that I should not have been glad of a friend like yourself at my back. What is the matter? Do you want me to give you a character? You have only to mention it."

" I do not want you to do me any favour that I could not return, Despard."

" That is being too scrupulous. The fashion now is to return nothing—not even an affront; so, you see, you are **safe**, Tommy, if you are in a spiteful humour after your four months' chase."

" **Despard, have you any conscience left?**"

" Hush. Yes, a little—against a rainy day. It pays duty abroad, so one keeps it quiet. Have you run through all yours already, that you are reduced to borrow mine?"

" No chaff just now, if **you** please. I am serious, I assure you."

" **And** very becoming it is. Quite impressive. And you could not **have** chosen a more suitable **spot**. It is **very** serious work being here without money."

" Which is your case wherever you go, I fancy, judging by the character you left behind you in most places."

" What a comfort **to have a** budding Boswell like yourself, to go on one's **track**, gleaning up the pleasing traits of one's disposition for a future biography! I am not ashamed of my honest poverty, Tommy. I shall be very glad if you can lend me a hundred francs to pay my hotel bill."

"Come, Jack, I will make a bargain with you. Answer me honestly, without any nonsense, and I will not let you be uncomfortable for want of five pounds, or even ten, if necessary."

"Take care, Tommy. If you offer too much, you will tempt me to be too accommodating with my answers. Before we begin, suppose you tell this *garçon* what you would like to have, as he is trying to catch your eye, with a perseverance worthy of the House of Commons."

Compton ordered coffee and cognac, and then drew closer to his companion. "I have seen Mrs. Atterbury, Despard."

" Have you? I wish I had. How was she looking?"

" Almost broken-hearted."

" Then I am glad I have not. Poor thing! Broken hearts do not kill, now-a-days."

" No; so to help it out, she was working on housemaid's wages, and has every appearance of going into a decline. And now, to add to all this, you see what has happened to her husband."

" Yes, I saw that. Poor Fred! He had better have stayed with Uncle Sam."

" Now, Despard, I have only one question to ask you ; and by your answer, I shall know whether to depend on your sincerity or not. What could induce you to make use of Mrs. Atterbury's name to get that money from me?"

Despard was silent a few minutes, before he answered, " A choice of evils, Tommy. Either I must have gone to jail, or I must have sold myself to the tempter, or I must have taken in the innocent. I chose the latter. I knew you were a good, honest boy, in spite of your conceit; and that you would never abuse the confidence you believed that poor lady had put in you. There you have the truth, and I am afraid it is all the interest you will get for your money."

"Well, I did think better of you than to suppose you would make a profit out of Eleanor Atterbury's misfortunes. I did think you had some feeling for her. I wish you had seen her as I did. It would haunt you to your grave, I can tell you that."

Despard hastily swallowed the brandy that had been placed before him. "Compton," he said, in a low, hoarse voice, "I can tell *you* this—her face *does* haunt me, night and day; and if I could serve her, I would. I *have* served her, more than she knows; for if I had gone to Martock, instead of to you——" He stopped, as if afraid of going too far, and put his hand to his head with a quick gesture of pain. Compton asked if he was well. Well? as well as a fellow could be, who was all to pieces, racked with neuralgia, and losing his sight. "I am not a quarter the man I was, Tommy, and that is the truth; if I were, I should be up and bestirring myself for Fred and his wife. But I have run fast, and it is the pace that kills. What is Martock about, have you heard?"

"His name does not appear at present."

"That is a bad sign. Do you think anything would induce Eleanor Atterbury to trust me again?"

"That I cannot say. But I am sure she bears no malice, and if you can suggest anything to serve her husband, I can promise it shall be made worth your while."

N 2

"What a keen hand you are becoming, Tommy, now you are grown serious. You say to yourself, 'Jack Despard never cares for anything but his own interest, therefore it will be better worth my while to spend a little money in getting out of him all he knows, than to argue with him on his past enormities, or even to tell him to his face he is a rogue.' I am not quite sure that you are right, remember; but, for a beginner, it does you credit. Come, I have had enough of this. Are you alone?"

"I have a party of acquaintance here."

"Let us go and join them, then, or they will be for tearing my grey hairs out of my head. They are getting uncommonly grey, Tommy. I am going down hill fast."

"Don't say that—we will pull you up again; never too late to mend, you know," said Compton, whose good nature had already

yielded to the old influence, to the rapid ex-
tinction of his resentment. He introduced Mr.
Despard to his friends, and they were so much
charmed with his conversation, that it was
agreed they should meet early the next day,
and do all their sight-seeing under his guidance.
Young Blatherwick, moreover, at Mr. Despard's invitation, walked with him to his hotel,
and stayed there, playing écarté till one o'clock
—a circumstance which was told to Compton
the next morning as a good story. He, having
his own opinion on the subject, looked grave,
and taking Sam apart, gave him to understand,
that though his friend Despard was a gentlemanly, pleasant fellow enough, he did not recommend any one to be too intimate with him,
and certainly not to try him at écarté, or anything in the way of play. "For an old hand
like myself, who know him, and am up to all
that sort of thing, it may be all very well; for

those who come to him fresh, it is not safe. He sees sharper under that blue shade of his than most men would with a microscope."

"Much obliged to you, Compton," said young Blatherwick, who, already intensely disgusted by the favour shown to his rival, had no idea of being supposed to want his advice. "If your friend is not safe company, I wonder you introduce him."

"As to that, when I introduce one gentle-man to another, I do not undertake to be re-sponsible for either of them. You may be the sharper of the two, of course, in which case, Jack must take care of himself. I only give you warning, that though one of the pleasantest fellows living, he is a deal too clever for most people, and I think will prove so for you—and now you may do as you please."

Blatherwick chose to follow his own counsel, and the result may be inferred from the fact that there was a very stormy scene between him and his uncle, and that Mr. Despard declined Compton's offer of money. When he was in want of it, he would remind him that he was, so to speak, in his debt—not till then. It was a comfort to have something in reserve, besides conscience, which was not always convertible. Compton saw how it was, but he could not help it; having written, at Despard's request, to beg Mr. Shannon would come over as soon as possible, he chose to await his arrival, and it was evident the movements of the whole party depended on his own. Mrs. Cummings professed to have taken quite a passionate fondness, as she said, for the dear old romantic streets; she could spend hours (not that she ever stayed more than two minutes) in contemplating those grand façades in the *Grande Place*; and the pulpit in Ste. Gudule was a thing to dream of—or under, as Mr. Prynne

would suggest in his droll way, persisting he
could cut out something twice as good as all
that gingerbread, with a sixpenny knife. All
this enthusiasm amounted to neither more nor
less than a resolve not to go away while the
petted favourite of society honoured Belgium's
capital with his presence; especially as she
owned to him—not without a pang—that she
had made the painful discovery that young
Mr. Blatherwick was not the young man with
whom she could trust the happiness of her dear
child. She could overlook a great deal, but if
he could gamble away his money at cards, she
should never know a moment's peace. For
Mrs. Cummings, it may be observed, like many
other people, considered the sin of gambling
to consist in losing your own money—not in
winning that of other people. So they all remained together, making the best of the intense
heat; and Compton, while waiting for Mr.

Shannon's arrival, had so little to do, that he divided the interval between wooing Sophy, and nursing Despard.

The latter had not exaggerated his infirmities; he was a mere wreck now, in body, as he had long been in spirit and soul—a last remnant of what had been strength and life, struggling against mortal decay in the one case as in the other, and, alas! with rapidly decreasing power. The young man shuddered at the double ruin, in one he had so unconsciously admired and followed; and pondered over the sermon he *saw*, as he had never done over any he heard. He was beginning to feel differently about many things. He was ashamed to think he could ever have meant to trifle with a nice girl like Sophy, who was evidently so fond of him, and so much too good for a conceited, self-opinionated fellow like Sam Blatherwick; and he began to draw pleasant pictures in his

mind, of country life, and domestic cheerfulness, and long evenings at home, with lots of
friends and cousins always coming to stay,
"and all that sort of thing"—much jollier,
after all, than the endless bother and racket of
London.   When once this affair of poor Fred's
was done with, he really thought he should
like to get married at once.

Mr. Shannon arrived at last, and was received by Compton alone, with eager inquiries
after Mrs. Atterbury. She was better, and
begged to be warmly and gratefully remembered to him. The message made his eyes
glisten, and he could not resist the temptation
of dilating on the exertions he had made, the
prudent things he had done, the sensible con-
clusions he had come to, till the lawyer cut him
short with a request to see Mr. Despard at
once, as time was precious.

" Don't think him quite as bad as he makes

himself appear," said Compton, as he went up to show him the room. "To hear him talk, one would suppose he had no feeling for anybody, and I really think he has for Mrs. Atterbury."

"He has proved it," said Mr. Shannon, shrugging his shoulders.

He had not much faith in the errand on which he had come, and had only obeyed the summons from the conviction that no chance ought to be lost. But Despard was too much in earnest to talk to a sensible man of business as he did to Compton; he went into facts directly, and they were of a nature to rivet the attention of his hearer.

"I always knew," he said, after going over sundry details for which we have no space, "that the old man was in Martock's power, and trembled at the lifting of his finger; but I never got at the real reason. It was a threat hung perpetually over our heads, after his death, that something might come out which would be utter disgrace; but what that was we could only conjecture. That evening that I watched for Mrs. Atterbury on Martock's premises, I saw her stand for a moment at the window with a large packet in her hand—she seemed to hesitate a moment, and then threw it behind her, and sprang out into the garden. My curiosity was so strong, that I let her pass, knowing Compton would see her as she went out. I got in by the window she had left open, and found the packet on the floor. I had so often schemed how to get at Martock's secrets, that I had no scruples about opening it. Spare me your comments—I have so many worse sins to answer for, this one sits lightly on my conscience."

"Pray, sir, go on; your conscience is not in my keeping."

" Some people would say you had missed a good sinecure; but we have no time to waste on old bon-mots. I opened the packet, and found so many papers and letters of old Mr. Atterbury's, dating years back, that I was obliged to abandon my first idea of searching them there, and carry them off with me—first burning the thick envelope, which I threw in the grate, and as it was half full of papers already, it raised such a smother and smoke, I was glad to be off undiscovered. Of course he would miss the packet, and the chances were he would think it had been burnt."

" Sagaciously judged; he did think so, and accused Mrs. Atterbury of doing it. Finding her innocent, he has been trying to detect the author of the mischief ever since. The only wonder is, that he has been so quiet about it."

"No wonder at all. When you read those letters, which I give into your keeping as evidence, you will see that he had no wish their contents should be made public. I do not believe he ever intended to do more than threaten. I do not think now, that he meant Atterbury to be brought to trial at all."

"I agree with you there. Go on."

"It is a sad story, and Frederick will want a great deal of courage to face it. His father was in great secret difficulty, many years ago, from an unsuccessful speculation, and saved himself by forging a deed, enabling him to dispose of a large sum belonging to his wife— all her property, in fact, that was not secured by settlement. Happily for her, she died without finding it out, but Martock, who was employed by her trustees, discovered it soon after, and, from that time, never let go his hold of the wretched man till he had drained him of money, credit, honour, and life. Read those letters, and tell me if they do not make your blood boil, old as you are; it made mine, and

I am older than you—in constitution, though not in years. Over and over again was that miserable wretch forced to do things he abhorred—forced to pay sums that ruined him—forced to commit frauds that ruined others—forced even to rob his own son—it is all there, told in such piteous language, that even that son can only forgive him for his sufferings. No, Martock never meant those letters to be seen; he only held them as an instrument of terror, as you would level a gun at a mob, that, once fired, would lose its charm. Put him in the witness-box, and these papers in a sharp counsel's hands; and if he survives the operation, it will be in such a state, that none of us need trouble ourselves about punishing him further."

"One thing more, Mr. Despard. What object had you in view in keeping these things by you?"

" Sir, I am speaking as if at your confessional. Secrets are money to a man in my circumstances. I often contemplated turning this to account, but the remnant of what was once the spirit of a gentleman, somewhere about me, prevented my carrying them to market. I drew on young Compton, that was all—and that only under severe pressure. I know I could have got money from Martock, if I had negotiated with him—but that I would not do. And now, I have only to say, there they are for you to do what you please with them. I owe Mrs. Atterbury more amends than this, and if she can ever bring herself to send me a word of forgiveness, I shall feel easier, but it is more than I dare ask. If these letters help to clear her husband, perhaps she will."

"If they do that, indeed——"

"They will go a long way towards it. All that will be brought against Frederick was done, if done at all, before he was in the firm; he never knew half that I did. And the letters throw light on many papers that puzzled us before. They are valuable in themselves, but still more so, when read as a commentary. Go carefully over all that the old man left behind him—if they have escaped Martock's clutches—and then I need not teach a gentleman of your acuteness what you should do next. I wish I could help you, but my sight is going fast, like many other good things I have wasted. Tell Atterbury from me, my last advice is, to forget all the rest I ever gave him. He is young enough to begin life afresh —I am not."

"I am sorry to hear you say so. Let me hope you are mistaken. No man with his reasoning powers still left him, need ever despair of amendment."

" That is a mild way of putting it, but I

suppose it is true, and that mine are gone; for I can no more do without play, than an opium-eater without his drug. It is become a necessary of life, and when it comes to that, you will agree with me the life is hardly worth having."

"I am no preacher, sir," said Mr. Shannon, gravely; "it is not for me to teach you what you know as well as I do. You have your Bible in your hands, and while life lasts, there is hope—even for you."

He put the papers into his pocket, retired to his own apartment, and shut himself up there for the remainder of the day. Compton made several attempts to obtain admission, but to no purpose; and it was not till the following afternoon that he succeeded in waylaying him just as he was going out.

"Well?" he said, impatiently, linking his arm in that of the lawyer, and walking on with

him uninvited, " well ?   Was I right in sending for you ?"

" Quite right."

" Is he as bad as he makes himself out ?"

" I hope not, for his own sake; and for
yours, I hope you will not have much more to
do with him."

" Oh, *I* understand him—but I am afraid
that youngster you saw me talking to, just
now, has been rather fleeced.   I gave him fair
warning, so it is not my fault."

" And I give you fair warning too ; though,
like most lads, you will think it a great affront.
Keep away from all such friends as if they had
the plague; show him kindness, if you like ;
allow him something, if you think he wants
it; but shut your ears to his precepts, and
your eyes to his example.   No wonder young
Atterbury was ruined, with such an evil genius
at his elbow."

"He has a good one to counterbalance it, sir—with such a wife."

"She is a good, patient, loving woman, certainly; and she has done all she could; but they have nearly killed her among them. However, as the evil influence has had its full turn, and done its worst, we may hope now the good will have a chance."

"When do you go back to England?"

"To-morrow morning."

"Then you will dine with me to-day. They give capital dinners at our hotel, and there is an old gentleman who takes a keen interest in this case, and you may find him useful."

The dinner sounded the greater inducement of the two, and Mr. Shannon allowed himself to be persuaded. On their way to the hotel, they went to a reading-room to see if there were anything new in the papers; and were struck on entering by the evident excite-

ment of all present, not only among the English, but the various continental readers of the
Brussels daily journals. Above all other
sounds, Mr. Prynne's voice was distinctly audible, at its shrillest pitch, protesting it was
what he had always foreseen. You never did
understand how to deal with that country—
every system you tried was worse than the
last—you hadn't a man out there fit to meet
such a crisis, nor an officer who knew half as
much of his duty as a corporal in the French
line; it was all over with your credit and pres-
tige now, and the best thing that could happen
to you and to the people, would be, that the
whole concern should fall into the hands of
Russia.

"What is the matter? Another row with
China?" cried Compton, elbowing his way
through the crowd, and forcibly getting possession of the first English paper within reach.

" Hulloa, Mr. Shannon—I say, this is serious. Oh, the rascals ! I wish I were in the middle of them ! Look here."

His companion looked, and read with the thrill we can all remember, the fatal telegram, that gave 1857 its terrible place in England's history. The Indian mutiny had broken out.

CHAPTER V.

ELEËMON.

THE arrest of her husband, though an event for which her apprehensions might have prepared her, fell upon Eleanor Atterbury like a crushing blow, from which it seemed doubtful whether she would ever recover. An alarming return of her former unfavourable symptoms kept her friends in the deepest anxiety, nor was she able, for many weeks, to leave her room. Anne Clavering nursed her night and day; comforted her, strengthened her, bore her up in

her arms through the overwhelming tide of
anguish that seemed ready to make shipwreck
alike of body and mind, till the darkened faith
again grasped the invisible, and the meek
spirit resumed its trust in the mercy of the
Judge who doeth right. Life and reason were
once more spared, and she appeared again in
the loving circle of which she was now considered a cherished member; but only a shadow of her former self, with that fatal con-
sumptive delicacy of tint, justifying the warning of her medical attendant, that, though with
great care, and a mild climate, she might live
for some years, yet any great fatigue or excitement might carry her off with little prepara-
tion; and a winter in England would be her
sentence of death. The truth was not kept
from her, as it was thought right she should
know the urgent necessity for calmness and
resignation, and the result proved that the

measure was wise. She wished, she prayed that she might live; she fought against weakness and disease; she exercised herself in hourly self-control; refrained from everything that could excite strong emotion—yielded to every restriction dictated by anxious care—and seconded every attempt to give her strength, or save her suffering, as if she had been nursing another, not herself. Her scruples about remaining at Lawleigh were quickly talked down by her friends; and as she was forbidden, as yet, to remove to London, she thankfully accepted the shelter and rest that were to build her up for the work for which she would live. They were all become attached to her, and made her their first consideration; reverencing her grief for the living as if it had been for the dead. It was a grief that found little utterance: she could not talk about her husband in prison, or discuss the probable issue of his trial; but she bore his shame stamped on every feature as if it had been her own. Nothing had inured her to this; it was often as much as her courage could support at all; and though she could think of little else, it was a burden that no one could share. Mr. Clavering, however, accidentally touched on a subject that was of great use in relieving her mind. It had all along been his conviction that emigration was the only thing for Atterbury, as soon as he was released; and he was glad to find how warmly she agreed with him. It seemed a real comfort to her to talk of the future, ignoring the fearful contingency between; and to settle how, and when, they might sail for Australia, as soon as all this was over, just as if it were a mere consideration of time and convenience. She was never tired of listening to his directions for the voyage, his experiences in the olden days, and the changes that had come on since he first went out; nor of his advice about climate, habits, dress, ways and means in general, management of stock, treatment of soil, and such-like, which he was delighted to give, and in giving which many an hour was spent, that led to his becoming almost as fond of her as if she had been one of his own cherished race. He never hinted what he often thought—how little she was calculated to bear the exertion of a settler's life; the sea-voyage was to work wonders, and it became, by degrees, an assumed point in the family, that she would go, as a matter of course. She accustomed herself to speak of her long journey, and even commenced such preparations as were within her reach; though they chiefly amounted to making small remembrances for every one who had been kind to her; and when tired of needlework, or writing, she would endeavour,

as far as her feeble powers would permit, to
resume the little services to which she had
been accustomed. Her voice was gone, and
her fingers had lost their *verve* ; but she could
still bring the sounds from the instrument that
were so sweet to Arthur, and which often
solaced herself when heart-sickness was too
strong for fortitude. It was only sacred music
she played now; she apologised to him for the
want of variety, but all other, even the melodies
she had once loved best, had lost the power to
soothe or cheer. And then she heard, what
English reticence would otherwise have · kept
back, that he had grown to feel the same, and
found the music that spoke of the future, more
cheering than that which recalled the past.
Not that he was less cheerful than before; but
the eternal was hourly growing more real, as
the transitory slipped from his hold, and though
he would not have begun on such a subject,

the pleasure it gave him to continue it led to many a peaceful half-hour, in which they strengthened each other's hands for the unknown struggle that both knew could not be far off.

Sympathy and good will increased on all sides, as Mrs. Atterbury's story became known. Mr. Maberley, and other rich neighbours, sent kind inquiries, and presents of hot-house fruit; the Vicar was constant in his visits, and as the only one who could venture to talk to her of her husband, was an invaluable friend and support; letters, and offers of service, with kind reproaches for having avoided them so long, were constantly coming from friends and acquaintance; in short, if personal esteem could have comforted her, she had proofs enough — sometimes from very unexpected quarters. But, true wife that she was, one kind word about her husband outweighed a

volume about herself; and though sensible of
all the kindness of this demonstration of feeling, none of it was half as precious as one
of Edward Wilton's despatches to his uncle,
reporting the last opinion of the lawyers, with
the last news of the prisoner, and unconsciously
displaying how fast the interest in him that
had begun in generous compassion, was ripen-
ing into friendship and regard.

Many as had been the gifts of nature and
fortune that Atterbury had lost, the power of
winning hearts remained still his own. The
lead he had always taken among his peers,
from his schoolboy days upward, was not
owing to his reputed wealth, but to those
personal qualities that boys and men love to
look up to and follow; and which had dazzled
the eyes and the judgment of Eleanor Ormonde,
till her heart was too surely his for her to judge
him at all. And now, in his utter destitution

of all other wealth—humbled, almost crushed by his position—he won upon Wilton before either of them was aware, until there seemed some danger of Edward's forgetting his real faults, in his anxiety to see him delivered from an unjust accusation. He found himself contriving excuses and palliations for him which Atterbury never thought of making, and wrote as earnestly to his uncle on the injustice of not taking temptations and disadvantages of early training into account, as if kind-hearted Uncle Rupert had never trusted or made allowances for anybody in his life.

"He does not seem to care for himself; he is resigned to bear any punishment that may be considered an expiation," he wrote, in a letter that Eleanor soon knew by heart, "but he thinks of and mourns about his wife night and day; and his one hope is, that if they will allow him the chance, he may yet make her happy, and repay the kindness you have shown her. If unselfishness, humility, and earnest desire for amendment and restitution, can do anything to atone for the past, and give promise for the future, we need not despair of Frederick Atterbury, even if he has to go through a harder trial than he has realised yet."

Mrs. Atterbury was allowed to keep this letter; but another came later in the summer, that it was not thought expedient she should see. The first account of the mutiny had just been received when Wilton wrote:

"I find Atterbury is less sanguine than the lawyers. They think he will come through; but he owns so much was done that he never half understood, that he is far from convinced they may not prove him implicated in matters of which he knows nothing. If he is con- demned, he prays you and Anne to watch over his wife, until **Mr. Ormonde** can be communicated with: he has little doubt he will make liberal arrangements on her behalf, if he does not come over to England to see after her himself. I am sorry to say, on inquiring to-day at that gentleman's agents', they had heard a very sad report that either he, or some of his family, had fallen victims to this dreadful outbreak. I trust it may not be true, but a day or two must bring more particulars. Keep this from Mrs. Atterbury till the truth is known."

The truth was made public only too soon. Mr. Ormonde's family were among the earliest victims of a fanaticism that knew no distinction of age, sex, or character; the accidental circumstance of his being away from home at the time, saved his own life—a deliverance that appeared to the childless and desolate man more of a scourge than a blessing. He

was reported as seriously ill, and more than
one speculation was raised among those inte-
rested in Eleanor's fate, as to what extent she
would be affected by any serious termination
of his disorder.

Eleanor mourned for her slaughtered kin-
dred, and still more for the affliction of the
generous relative to whose assistance she
owed, among other things, the means of her
husband's defence. The appalling details were
kept from her as much as possible, but she
knew enough to haunt her pillow, and so
visibly affect her nerves, that her medical
adviser altered his mind, and recommended
change of scene, even at the cost of pure air.
Change of scene to her, of course meant
London. If she might travel at all, she must
be near Frederick till all was over, and the
question of locality was still under discussion,
when a letter unexpectedly arrived that brought

the matter to a point. Her old hostess, Miss Craggs, having discovered her whereabout, begged to inform her she had still some pro- perty of hers in her keeping, if she would please to say how and where it should be sent; and took the liberty, at the same time, of men- tioning that she had most desirable lodgings to let, in a salubrious part of London, where ladies or gentlemen could be accommodated on reasonable terms, as per advertisement enclosed. The address was very near the spot where Eleanor's heart was treasured; and she at once expressed a wish that the lodgings might be secured. She owed Miss Craggs a good deal for unbought kindness in her hour of need, as well as for subsequent injury received on her account, and the situation was just what she wished—only it would not be agree- able for Anne. This last remark being what Miss Clavering never chose to attend to, was not repeated; and to Miss Craggs's salubrious lodgings they soon after removed—Anne, Eleanor, and Nurse Moyle, who by this time had acquired as despotic a sway over Mrs. Atterbury, as if she had been brought up in her dominions, and petted and scolded her by turns, almost as lovingly as if she had been of Clavering blood. Uncle Rupert went backwards and forwards by rail as often as he could, and Edward Wilton's leisure hours were of course devoted to them entirely. The Sydneys hoped to be in town at a friend's house during the trial; indeed, everybody who had ever been acquainted with either husband or wife, was equally determined, if possible, to enjoy the excitement, which even when your friends are in danger, is not without its charm.

There was a weary interval of waiting, through long, stifling days, before the trial began, but that was little to endure in comparison of the length of the trial itself. In their womanly ignorance, they had formed no conception of this, and the sickness, not only of hope deferred, but of fear getting the upper hand, made it a season of great suffering to all concerned. We have nothing to do with the details of the proceedings; it has not been the men that work, but the women that weep, that our story has followed all along, and it remains with them still.

All that friends and legal advisers could do for Atterbury, was zealously and skilfully done, and, thanks to the light Despard had thrown, with good hopes of success; but nothing could prevent his trial from being as sore a punishment as his utmost fortitude could endure. Repent as he might, his wrongdoing must bear its fruit, and that fruit he must gather, in all its bitterness. But there

was a keener torture than this, which he had
dreaded from the first—the severest that a
man could stand and bear—that of hearing his
father's name held up to obloquy, without the
power—without the right, of uttering a word
in his defence. His lawyers did all they
could, but facts spoke for themselves. He
had foreseen it would be so, and he had to
bear it, but it was an agony beyond all anti-
cipation, and such as even the most prejudiced
of his audience could not witness without respect and pity.

Mr. Clavering was as much touched as his
nephew by the manner in which he went
through this ordeal. The shame cast on himself—the exposure to the eyes of all his acquaintance—the consciousness of being the
topic of all the papers, moved him comparatively little: it was almost a satisfaction to
offer this poor atonement for the sorrows he

had helped to cause: but for his dead father
and his living wife, his anguish was too great
for fortitude or resignation. Nothing could remove the dishonour from the memory of the
one—would any time be allowed him to heal
the broken heart of the other?

It was a calm autumn day—tolerably clear,
even in that dim street; and two ladies sat together in Miss Craggs's first-floor drawing-room,
nominally engaged in needlework, but in such
a restless state of watchfulness, it may be
doubted if half a dozen stitches were made in
half an hour. These were Anne Clavering
and Mrs. Tresham — the only two friends
whom Eleanor could bear near her at this
crisis. When she first came to town, she had
shrunk from seeing any one, but Mrs. Tresham's urgent entreaty for admission prevailed,
and when they had once met, she was never

denied to her again. She seemed to cling to
these two—the two to whom Atterbury had
caused the deepest grief—as if she felt their
pardon, their prayers, would serve him best in
his need; and if she had sought the world
over, she could not have found another two,
who would have sympathised more deeply,
or attended her with more loving solicitude.
From the first day of the trial, Mrs. Tresham
never left her, except to return home at night;
and by their united care she was saved from
all rude contact with the outer world, and the
comparative quiet secured that was essential
to her over-taxed brain.   The cards that piled
the table testified to the respect shown her by
the world, and many kind proposals had been
sent, that she should remove to the better accommodation the inviters pressed on her ac-
ceptance; but she had declined all. And on
this day, when they had reason to expect the

verdict would be given, she had been unable to endure even the society of her companions; and had silently retired to her bedroom, to pass the interval on her knees. Mrs. Tresham, not being quite easy at this, followed softly, to make sure she was not ill, but came back immediately, without being observed.

"She is praying," she said to Anne, in a whisper.

"She does little else," was Miss Clavering's reply, and the tears fell from the eyes of both. They sat together and waited; speaking now and then with hushed voices, as if too near something holy for anything but reverence. Presently, there was a tap at the door. Every sound made them start, though this was only a summons Mrs. Tresham was half expecting, and she went down directly to receive her son and Charles Lyle.

"How is she, mother?" was Herbert's first

greeting. He looked flushed and excited, as if he could not keep still for a minute.

" As well as we could hope. Very patient."

" What does she do with herself all this time? I should go mad."

" So might she, dear, if she were as impetuous as you. She does the only thing she can; she trusts, and prays. Oh, how shall we tell her if our fears come true ?"

" Look here, mother. Lyle and I are going to the court now, to get the first intelligence. If it is bad, he will bring it—he will know how — I couldn't: if it is all right, I shall come. I want to be the one to tell her good news."

" My boy, I wish you would have come to see her before. She has never said a word of blame for what you did."

" That makes it all the worse. Never mind. If Atterbury is condemned, I shall be off—I don't know where, and it does not much matter, but I shall never hold up my head again. Well! we are off now, and remember, if you see Lyle coming, prepare for the worst."

" You choose him a sad office," said his mother, as she pressed the tall curate's hand; " it is just like him to accept it, but God forbid he should have it to do."

She came up again, and sat down with Anne, as we described them just now, trying to work, but doing nothing but listen. Time passed, and they were beginning to wonder whether there would really be any news at all that day, when a noise below, unusual in that house, made them both run to the top of the stairs, listen for a moment, and then hurry down.

The narrow hall seemed full of people, and Miss Craggs, who appeared to have just come in, was giving orders to one person to run for the nearest doctor, and to the others to "bring him in and lay him on the sofa." Some one, prone and helpless, was being borne into the parlour by two gentlemen, in one of whom Anne recognised young Compton. She called him eagerly by name, and as soon as he was relieved of his charge, he flew to obey her summons.

"Don't come down; you can do nothing; she knows him—she will do what is necessary till the doctor comes. I am afraid he is very bad."

"Who is it?"

"Did you not see? It is old Martock. Mind Mrs. Atterbury does not hear. It would give her a shock. How is she, Miss Clavering?"

"As well as patience can make her. Tell me, what has happened?"

" Hush—come a little more this way. Did you read the account of his cross-examination ?"

" Yes, of course."

" Well, it was too much for him—no wonder. I never saw a man made such an example of, and so forced to convict himself out of his own mouth. The sensation in court was tremendous, and he took it terribly to heart—went home quite ill, and was ordered severe remedies, and to keep quiet. But no, nothing would prevent his coming to hear the end. His clerk told me this morning he had been like a madman with rage; and he persisted in saying the prisoner *must* be found guilty, and he *would* be there. He had done his best to get a verdict against him—that we all knew. He staid through the judge's summing up—heard some splendidly cutting remarks on himself, and, when the jury retired, he tried to get out of the crowd; some of them knew and hooted him; and when he got into the air, he fell down in this fit. A gentleman who was waiting, as I was, to hear the result, helped me to pick him up, and Miss Craggs being there too, on the same errand, begged us to bring him to her house."

" Yes, ma'am," said Miss Craggs, who passed at that moment with a basin and warm water, " it isn't that I owe him any gratitude, for I don't; he used me downright shameful, considering that my mother was a faithful servant of his, for next to no wages, and finding herself in everything, for years and years; and if it hadn't been for the Lord's goodness, and an old aunt's legacy last Christmas, I might have been in the workhouse now, thanks to him. But I'm a Christian, I hope, and I've no objection to be thought so, and the poor sinner shall not die for want of coals of fire on his head, if I can help it. Brandy, sir, did you ask for? I keep no spirits in my house. I am a total abstainer from spirituous liquors in any form. If you can't keep life in without brandy, it's my belief you had better let it alone."

There was no time to argue this knotty point, as the surgeon arrived at that moment, and the patient had to be put to bed. With great difficulty consciousness was restored, and the first word he uttered was the name of Eleanor Atterbury.

"He can't see her, poor lady," pronounced Miss Craggs; "she has had enough of him in her time, and she is not equal to such a scene just now."

The sick man turned his eyes sternly on the speaker, and with an effort that showed his mind was, for the moment, under his control, murmured, "I must."

" Is she here ?" asked the surgeon.   " It is
very bad for him to be thwarted;" as, indeed, the restless twitching of the clothes, and
clutching of the withered hands at vacancy,
too plainly showed.   The strange gentleman,
a dignified, handsome man, in deep mourning,
came forward from the side of the bed, where
he had been silently attending on the patient,
and asked, in a low voice, if Mrs. Frederick
Atterbury was in the house ?

" Yes, sir, she is," said Miss Craggs; " but
nobody can see her, unless it be indeed by
medical orders, in which case I say nothing,
of course, never thinking it right to set up my
judgment against the doctor's."

"Bring her to me," said the voice from the
bed.   There was such a strange solemnity in
the slow, solemn tones, that all present
listened with fear.   Compton went to consult
Miss Clavering, still lingering on the staircase;

but before they could decide, the door over-
head opened quickly, and Eleanor came down,
looking so terrified by the strange sounds she
had heard, that Anne was obliged to tell her
the truth directly. She had imagined something so much more dreadful, that, shocked as
she was, it was comparatively a relief, and she
went instantly to the sick man's bed.

"I am sorry to see you like this, Mr.
Martock. Is there anything I can do for
you?"

He fixed his dull eyes on the young face
whose bloom he had helped to wither; and
made a desperate effort to speak—though
what he would have said, no one ever knew.
Consciousness remained, and the wish and the
will to do something — distressing, almost
terrible to see—but the long misused power
was gone for ever, and though his eyes gazed
at Eleanor, in almost supplicating agony, they

could do nothing more. She bent over him, she put her ear to his lips, she tried to read his signs; for she knew well how fearfully valuable these moments were, and would have done anything to give him the opportunity his eyes seemed to implore. "Can you follow us if we pray for you?" she said, finding all her efforts fruitless; "can you make a sign to show you throw yourself on the Saviour's mercy?"

Alas! for that, too, the hour was past. His eyes closed, and made no sign.

"You had better retire, madam," said the surgeon, at last, gently removing her from the bedside. "He can neither see nor hear you now, and cannot last many hours."

She yielded, so faint with the agitation of such a scene, that she could hardly see or hear herself at the moment. She did not know that Anne and Mrs. Tresham had already quitted the room, nor did she observe that Compton courteously made way for the stranger, as he advanced with the air of one who had a right to accost her, and drew her arm in his. She clung to him for support, and he was rather alarmed to feel how she trembled.

"God forgive him—God forgive him as I do!" she repeated, as if thinking aloud, hardly aware that she was overheard. "Oh! to see death like this!—how should we meet it if it came on us so suddenly?"

The arm on which she leant trembled as much as her own.

"There have been those, as young as you, to whom it has been a passage to glory," he returned, in a low voice, that seemed strangely familiar; but before she could even conjecture why it was, he went on to inquire gravely, what the invalid had been to her? "I can see he was not your friend."

Q 2

"He was the only man I ever feared—the first who taught me what it was to have an enemy. I have dreaded so often what he might yet do—and now——"

"He will injure you no more. No enemy shall ever terrify you again—if I can prevent it."

She drew her arm from his, recollecting for the first time that she was speaking to a stranger. "Excuse me, sir, but I do not know why——"

She stopped short, looking at him in astonishment. Now that she could see his face, an undefined resemblance to the cherished image of her father made her heart bound with sudden hope. He held out both his hands, and his kind, sweet smile as he saw her thoughts, showed her she had hoped aright. "I did not mean to startle you, or, indeed, to intrude at all just at present, but since we have met, Eleanor, let your cousin stand by you now; it may be a comfort to have one at hand who dearly loved your father."

"It *is* you, then, Mr. Ormonde! Oh, how I have thought of you—longed to see you—longed to give you comfort—and now you have come—at what a moment!"

"I know—I know," he said, drawing her to him affectionately, "we have both suffered enough to feel for each other, and come what may, I will never forsake you. Your home henceforth——"

He was interrupted by her start; there was a sound in the passage that made her hurry to the door. There stood Herbert Tresham, panting and breathless, and on either side of him, his mother and Anne. "Mrs. Atterbury!" he almost sobbed, seizing her hand, "Mrs. Atterbury! Will you forgive me for my news?"

She stood motionless; frightened by his violent agitation.

"You will believe me, won't you, that I would have undone my own work if I could? The fellow took me in—I was never more miserable in my life than when I found how I had been hoodwinked. I have hated myself ever since—I never dared come near you, till I brought something to make amends; and now, will you say you forgive me, and then I shall hold up my head again? Oh, mother—what is the matter? She does not speak!"

"You have startled her—she does not understand," said Mrs. Tresham. "Dear Mrs. Atterbury, my poor boy has run all the way to be the first to tell you all is happily over!"

"He is saved, saved, Eleanor," whispered Anne, passing her arm round her waist, and kissing her cheek, "saved to make you happy for many a year, I trust. So bravely as you

have borne sorrow, try and be courageous
against joy!"

She did her best; she struggled to be calm
and glad, but her brain was too dizzy to realise anything, and she never knew how long
the interval was, nor how it passed, between
the moment of her hearing of her husband's
acquittal, and that of her finding herself up-
stairs, with her head resting on his bosom.

Mr. Ormonde lost no time in conveying his
young relations to more comfortable apart-
ments. Childless and wealthy, his heart had
yearned over Eleanor, as one of the last of his
race; and it was chiefly on her account, that,
as soon as his health would permit, he had
hastened over to England. Her letter had
reached him just before his own calamity; and
when he was so ill as to doubt of his recovery,
he had borne her petition in mind, and stirred

up his friends to work for hers. In consequence of this, she had the comfort of announcing to Mrs. Tresham a promise of a chaplaincy for Charles Lyle; and of arranging, to their mutual satisfaction, the terms on which she was to receive the children of a rich and liberal gentleman, who had empowered Mr. Ormonde to do so at once. The remuneration being in proportion to his station and requirements, would go far towards restoring to the widow the comforts she had lost; and though the idea of sending Clara to India made her shudder, yet, as the young people themselves rejoiced, she could not but enter into their joy, and prepare with a thankful heart for her new and welcome duties.

If Mr. Ormonde could have kept his kinswoman near him, he would have given up India entirely, and made any sacrifice to enable Atterbury to live in England. But the advice of both physician and lawyer was hostile to such a hope. A British winter must be avoided for the wife—an idle life for the husband. On this latter point Atterbury was resolute. Any assistance towards satisfying his creditors, and enabling him to begin work with a prospect, however distant, of success, he would thankfully accept; he did not care what the work was, nor where it was, so long as the climate suited Eleanor ; but nothing should induce him to go on eating the bread of another, or spend an hour longer in idleness than he could possibly help. No one could deny that he was right, and a long sea voyage being pronounced as Eleanor's best chance, the result of much anxious discussion was the adoption of Mr. Clavering's plan: they were to go to Australia.

Atterbury's sufferings had not left him unscathed. He was an altered man; his youth and his recklessness were gone alike, and he never could forget how he had stood to hear his father's honour blasted, and only barely saved his own. The anguish inflicted on that father by his enemy, never really understood till the revelations of the trial, had so deeply stung the son, that it was with vengeance in his heart he left his prison; palpitating with keen desire to punish the man who had caused such unutterable misery. It was no small shock to be taken by Mr. Clavering into the darkened room, where the dreaded enemy lay, and to hear how terrible a vengeance had already fallen, without his lifting a hand. Passion and indignation were disarmed in that silent presence, and he owned with contrite humility that it was only of God's mercies that he, too, had not utterly fallen, as, but for Eleanor, he must have done long ago.

The tone of public opinion had so changed of late, that not only was there a strong demon-

stration of sympathy for the wife, whose conduct had been pronounced, on high authority, as
beyond praise, but Mr. Ormonde's endeavours
to arrange Frederick's affairs were readily met,
and as a large pecuniary sacrifice was offered,
no opposition was made to his plan of emigration. It was necessary, if they went at all,
that they should go soon, to save Mrs. Atterbury
from the approaching season, and their passage
was secured in a vessel that was to sail the end
of November. They were to take out letters
from Rupert Clavering to his partner, and
Atterbury was looking forward to the freedom
and adventures of a farming life. Eager to be
doing something, to be repaying some part of
his obligations, the exile from his native land
appeared a slight evil to those from which he
had escaped, and the only prospect he could
not face without flinching, was the uncertainty
of Eleanor's health.

Mr. Martock's death was not without its

consequences to many. The wealth he had
amassed, but never enjoyed, passed into the
hands of a nephew, a plain, upright man in the
north of England, who had never received a
sixpence from his uncle, and was not at all prepared, either for the large inheritance, or the
obloquy that accompanied it. He did his best
to remove the stain, by refunding such sums
as he could discover to have been iniquitously
obtained; and Atterbury's creditors, among
others, reaped the benefit of this integrity.
The unhappy debtors of Mr. Martock, of whom
there was a melancholy list in his private
books, were also the better for the change, Sir
John Pierpoint being among the number. The
extent to which he had been shackled, hand
and foot, was palliation enough of his conduct
to win Eleanor's pardon; and for her sake,
Mr. Ormonde extended to him a generous assistance, to which he by no means considered
him entitled.

Mrs. Atterbury never recovered the rest of her trinkets. Adam contrived to elude all attempts at his apprehension. The story told by Lockwood about the bracelet was true in all its essential points, and the bracelet itself had come into the hands of the police the very day that Herbert sent for him. The narrow escape from detection at the pawn-broker's probably made him more wary, for nothing was learned of his fate till two or three years later, when Mr. Clavering heard of a man answering his description having died of a lingering complaint in an hospital in Liver-pool, who expressed great penitence for his past sins, and had only one article in his possession that showed signs of his having seen better days—a small clasped Bible, in a bind-ing that had been handsome once, in whose fly-leaf were the initials in a clear, womanly hand, E. M. A.

The engagement of Sophia Cummings with

Mr. Compton was nearly settled before they left Brussels, and was now an acknowledged fact. How young Blatherwick bore it, nobody seemed to think it necessary to inquire, as his uncle seemed perfectly satisfied. Mrs. Cummings could not thwart her darling child, and took the man of Sophia's heart at once into her own. She did more, she took him into her house too—a house in a well-sounding street in town, whither she had repaired with her whole family for the winter, and where, in the most pressing terms, she invited her aunt and Arthur to pay her a visit. For the sake of seeing more of Mrs. Atterbury, they consented; and under Compton's genial superintendence, there was no fear now of their being victims of careful management. He and his mother-in-law elect were on the best terms imaginable, each firmly believing in the blind submission of the other—a happy state of things, which one **could** only hope would last.

"Times are changed with me now," said Eleanor to Anne, one day, when the latter had been arranging a variety of matters connected with her outfit, for which she herself had no strength; "it seems almost strange that others should be working so diligently at my wardrobe, when Mrs. Compton that is to be has so much of my handiwork in hers. I hope Milly will go on improving; she was here this morning, and very affectionate and kind. I have been writing to Mrs. Fenton. She has forgiven me by this time for my want of confidence. If her husband does carry out that plan he mentioned yesterday when he called, of accepting a church in our colony, I may be able to return some of their kind hospitality: only they must not put it off too long."

Anne stopped in her employment of filling a neat work-box with materials, and sitting down by her friend, rebuked the words by a caress.

" Nay, I am not morbid, or frightened about myself. I know I cannot live long, but I am in loving Hands, and shall be as near heaven there as here, or at quiet, peaceful Lawleigh. Think of me sometimes there; I have given you trouble enough to prevent my being easily forgotten. I can never, never repay you—that is impossible; but living or dying, I shall love you, thank you, always. You know," she continued, after a short silence, " our last arrangement—that Herbert Tresham goes out with us ?"

" Edward was telling me this morning. He thinks it will be the saving of him, especially under your husband's eye, as he is too rash and easily led to be trusted alone."

" And Mr. Wilton is just the man to trust my husband. He knows him as if they had been friends for years. Frederick looks on Herbert as a sacred charge already, and if ever one brother watched another, he will watch him."

" And who will watch you, if you are ill on the voyage ? You may be right in refusing to take a maid, but I own I am anxious about your comfort."

" I forgot to tell you, I shall have a friend on board, who will do anything for me. Mr. Clavering has arranged it all. That poor Mrs. Mackay, whose husband's pardon he got in the winter, has been invited by a brother, who has made money in the gold-fields, to go out to him with her family, and as he has sent them the means, they will be our fellow-passengers, and she is to look after me if I require it. I saw her this morning, and if you had seen her delight at the idea of doing something for me, though we neither of us know what, you would have no fear of my being neglected."

"I have no fear of your not being loved by everybody. I am growing quite jealous of my uncle's fondness for you. He actually talks of going out himself next year, to wind up affairs, as he pretends, but I know it only means, to see if you are well and happy. I wonder what he thinks *I* am to do meanwhile!"

" Is it possible," thought Eleanor, " that she does not imagine ?"

She longed to speak her thoughts, but had not courage, nor was she certain that it would be wise. When alone once more with her friend Arthur, she gave vent to her earnest wish, that the two to whom she owed so much might be rewarded in each other.

" I wish it too," he said, "though as Wilton would never consent to be an idle gentleman,

and there is not employment for two at Lawleigh, it would cost us Miss Clavering's company,—a loss for which we **are ill** prepared.
But for her happiness one would put up **with**
worse evils, and I, for one, shall not miss either
of you long."

She put her hand **on** his, but made no reply.

"Yes," he went on, "we are both bound on
a long voyage, Mrs. Atterbury, and across a
stormy sea, but I think we shall meet when it
is over. You remember our favourite song:

> The friends gone before us,
> **At** home we shall find them.

It may be **hard to say** which will arrive
first, but the same hope will go with us, and
the same Father waits for us there. But for
the comfort of that belief, **I do not know** how
I could have parted with **such a friend** as you.
As it is, I shall hear nothing **so sweet** as your
music—until we meet again."

The last day came; the last preparations were completed, and Atterbury, who had been hard at work all the morning, came into his wife's room to see if there were anything she wanted him to do, but found her sitting at the table, so intent on an old drawing-book lying open before her, that she did not hear his entrance. He looked over her shoulder, and as she perceived he was near, their hands met in a close, meaning pressure. Well they both remembered the day when his pencil had traced those sketches, whose subject she had so little fathomed at the time; well could they both read the moral, of the burden borne in silence under the show of prosperity—the remorse transformed into penitence through the hope kindled by faithful love—the struggle with the powers of evil that urged to despair —the beckoning hand of mercy encouraging to proceed—all was clear to Eleanor now, clear as the belief deeply seated in her heart, that her bondsman **too** had been rescued by a miracle not the less gracious, because it is wrought every hour.

"One picture is still wanting, Frederick," she said, at last; "we ought to have the deliverance."

He drew the **paper** hastily to him, took a pencil from his travelling case, and sketched a group of three figures, of a beauty **that** surprised himself. Nature had meant him for an artist of no small power, and he **had** the gift of expressing a likeness with a few easy touches, that **so** often far exceeds elaborate portraiture. The humbled penitent's face was hidden in his hands, but that of the wife, **whose arm was** thrown over him as he knelt, was **turned to** heaven—calm, peaceful, and satisfied—while over her **was an** angel form, **extending a pitying hand** as if in benediction of both. It was only an outline, but there was no mistaking for whom they were meant; and gentle tears, such as that angel's self might have wept, fell from Eleanor's eyes on that graceful image of her rival—which she laid aside among her treasures, never to be parted with while she lived.

And so to their new home they sailed; he, chastened and saddened by the remembrance of the past, yet strong in hope, and earnest in purpose for the future; she, without a fear for the risks that she knew, or for those as yet untried, bearing that about with her that was more than country or home; finding all she desired of this world's good in her husband's presence—all her soul could ask or want in the Presence that went with her, and gave her rest.

Our tale is nearly told; the reader has long since foreseen all that yet remains to tell.

The dearest wish of Uncle Rupert's heart, next to the redemption of Lawleigh, was to see Edward and Anne united; but even his sanguine nature had at one time nearly abandoned hope. How soon they all began to hope again, it were hard to say; still harder to determine how and when Anne first ventured to read her own heart, and admit that what she had told herself was only cousinly regard, esteem, and friendship, had become affection, that craved the avowal she had once seemed to shun. We only know that his constancy and unselfishness deserved the reward, and that it proved even beyond his dearest anticipations. Their marriage, like everything else, brought its drawbacks with it: Wilton's home is necessarily in London, and Lawleigh sees its heiress only at intervals; but their happiness, when we heard of them last, was as pure as any earthly good can be;

and the memory of past trials bears the fruit it is ever meant to bear—the grateful sense of the guiding mercy, that ever makes a pathway for those that follow it, even through the DEEP WATERS.

THE END.

C. WHITING, BEAUFORT HOUSE, STRAND.

A

CATALOGUE OF BOOKS

PUBLISHED BY

CHAPMAN AND HALL,

193, PICCADILLY.

APRIL, 1863.

April, 1863.

A List of New Works & New Editions

PUBLISHED BY CHAPMAN & HALL.

THE FINE ARTS' QUARTERLY REVIEW.

In super royal 8vo., price Six Shillings per Number,

No. I. to appear in May.

———◦❈◦———

Part I. to be published May 1st.

To be completed in Twelve Parts, price Five Shillings each. :

THE FARM HOMESTEADS OF ENGLAND.

A Collection of Plans of English Homesteads existing in different Districts of the Country, Carefully selected from the most approved Specimens of Farm Architecture, to illustrate the Accommodation required under various modes of Husbandry; with a Digest of the Leading Principles recognised in the Construction and Arrangement of the Buildings.

Edited by J. BAILEY DENTON, M. Inst. C.E., F.G.S.,

Engineer to the General Land Drainage and Improvement Company.

———◦❈◦———

NEW NOVEL BY OWEN MEREDITH.

In 2 vols. post 8vo.

A NOVEL.

By OWEN MEREDITH. [*In May.*

———◦❈◦———

In 3 vols. post 8vo.

A NEW NOVEL.

By THOMAS ADOLPHUS TROLLOPE.
Author of 'Marietta,' &c. [*In May.*

———◦❈◦———

NEW NOVEL.

In 3 vols. post 8vo.

DEEP WATERS. A NOVEL.

By MISS ANNA DRURY.
Author of 'Misrepresentation,' 'Friends and Fortune,' &c.

  [*In April.*

———◦❈◦———

In crown 8vo.

STRANGE THINGS AMONG US.

By HENRY SPICER. [*In May.*

New and Cheaper Edition, post 8vo., with Illustrations,

CHILD'S HISTORY OF ENGLAND.

By CHARLES DICKENS. [*In May.*

In crown 8vo., Fourth Edition,

THE IRISH SKETCH-BOOK.

With Illustrations.

By W. M. THACKERAY. [*In May.*

NEW SPORTING NOVEL.

In 3 vols. post.

CHARLIE THORNHILL;

OR, THE DUNCE OF THE FAMILY.

By CHARLES CLARKE. [*In May.*

In 3 vols. post 8vo,

CARDINAL POLE;

OR, THE DAYS OF PHILIP AND MARY. AN HISTORICAL ROMANCE.

By W. HARRISON AINSWORTH. [*In June.*

In post 8vo.

BERTHA'S REPENTANCE.

By J. F. CORKRAN. [*In April.*

In 2 vols. post 8vo. The Second Series of

PICTURES OF GERMAN LIFE

IN THE EIGHTEENTH AND NINETEENTH CENTURIES.

By GUSTAV FREYTAG. Translated by Mrs. MALCOLM.

[*In April.*

New and Cheaper Edition, post 8vo.

THE DUTCH AT HOME

By ALPHONSE ESQUIROS. [*In May.*

A 2

In post 8vo. with Illustrations.

A VISIT TO RUSSIA IN THE AUTUMN OF 1862.

By HENRY MOOR.   [*In May.*

———◆◇◆———

In 3 vols. fcap. 8vo.

ROBERT BROWNING'S POETICAL WORKS.

New Edition, with Corrections and Additions.   [*In May.*

In May will be published the First Volume, containing LYRICS, ROMANCES, MEN AND WOMEN. This Edition will include the whole of the Author's Poems, contained formerly in 7 vols.

———◆◇◆———

In 3 vols. fcap. 8vo.

HENRY TAYLER'S POETICAL WORKS.

PHILIP VAN ARTEVELDE, &c.

New and Corrected Edition.   [*In the press.*

JUST PUBLISHED.

In fcap. 8vo. 5s.

THE GREEK CHRISTIAN POETS, AND THE ENGLISH POETS.

By ELIZABETH BARRETT BROWNING.

———◆◇◆———

Fcap. 8vo. 6s.

SELECTIONS FROM THE POEMS OF ROBERT BROWNING.

———◆◇◆———

New Edition, post 8vo. 7s. 6d., with Forty Illustrations.

OLIVER GOLDSMITH, A BIOGRAPHY.

By JOHN FORSTER.

———◆◇◆———

In demy 8vo., 14s., with Twenty-six Illustrations by 'Phiz.'

BARRINGTON.

By CHARLES LEVER.

JUST PUBLISHED.

MR. ANTHONY TROLLOPE'S NEW WORK.

In 2 vols. demy 8vo. price 22s.

ORLEY FARM.

By ANTHONY TROLLOPE.

With Forty Illustrations by J. E. MILLAIS, A.R.A.

In post 8vo., 10s. 6d.

TALES OF ALL COUNTRIES.

Second Series.

By ANTHONY TROLLOPE.

Author of ' Dr. Thorne,' ' Orley Farm,' &c.

Third Edition, in 2 vols. demy 8vo. 34s.

NORTH AMERICA.

By ANTHONY TROLLOPE.

' This book should be welcomed both for its subject and its author,—for this latest survey of the States is information on an engrossing topic, and it is information endorsed by a popular name. Mr. Trollope promised himself that he would write his own book about the United States as the ambition of his literary life, irrespective of their recent troubles. The circumstance that he has seen them seething in the cauldron of revolution, though not part of his original design, adds immensely to the animation and interest of the result.'—*Times.*

In demy 8vo. 18s.

THE LIFE OF LORD BOLINGBROKE,

SECRETARY OF STATE IN THE REIGN OF QUEEN ANNE,

By THOMAS MACKNIGHT.

' Mr. Macknight is successful in reviving in the reader's mind a very distinct image of Bolingbroke in all his grace, his force, and his reckless and insolent unscrupulousness ; and the various events of his career are illustrated and connected with an intelligent knowledge of the times, and with honesty and good sense.'—*Saturday Review.*

Second Edition, in 2 vols. post 8vo. 21s.

ROBA DI ROMA.

By WILLIAM W. STORY.

' Till Rome shall fall the City of the Seven Hills will be inexhaustible as a subject of interest. " Roba di Roma" contains the gatherings of an honest observer and a real artist. . . . . It has permanent value to entitle it to a place of honour on the shelf which contains every lover of Italy's Rome-books.'—*Athenæum.* [*In April.*

JUST PUBLISHED.

In 2 vols, post 8vo. 21s.

LIFE IN THE SOUTH FROM THE COMMENCEMENT OF THE WAR.

By A BLOCKADED BRITISH SUBJECT.

Being a Social History of those who took part in the Battles, from a Personal Acquaintance with them in their own Homes.

'The authoress has enjoyed great and unusual facilities for her work from a personal acquaintance with many of the leading men who took part in the battles . . . There is much in it calculated to throw light on the social condition and status both of the slaves and their masters in the South.'—*Observer*.

In demy 8vo. 14s.,

THE LIFE AND TIMES OF ST. BERNARD,

ABBOT OF CLAIRVAUX.

By J. COTTER MORISON.

'Mr. Morison writes in good honest English, clearly and forcibly, and worthy of his brilliant subject. . . . The book reads like a romance; and the career of the extraordinary man who is its central figure would be as literally impossible of the world of to-day as that of any of Alexander Dumas's heroes in the world of fact.'—*Saturday Review*.

In one large handsome folio volume, price 6s. 6d.

Published by authority of the Science and Art Department of the Committee of Council on Education.

SOUTH KENSINGTON MUSEUM.

ITALIAN SCULPTURES OF THE MIDDLE AGES AND PERIOD OF THE REVIVAL OF ART.

A Series of 50 Photographs of Works in the above Section of the Museum, Selected and Arranged

By J. C. ROBINSON, F.S.A.

The Photographs executed by C. THURSTON THOMPSON.

By Authority of the Committee of Council on Education.

In a handsome royal 8vo. volume, 7s. 6d.

THE ITALIAN SCULPTURE COLLECTIONS OF THE SOUTH KENSINGTON MUSEUM.

A Descriptive Catalogue, comprising an Account of the Acquisitions from the Gigli and Campagna Collections. Illustrated with 20 Engravings.

By J. C. ROBINSON, F.S.A., &c.,

Superintendent of the Art Collections of the South Kensington Museum.

[*April*, 1863.

A CATALOGUE OF BOOKS

PUBLISHED BY

CHAPMAN AND HALL,

193, PICCADILLY."

ADAMS — ROADS AND RAILS, AND THEIR PRAC-
TICAL INFLUENCE ON HUMAN PROGRESS, PAST, PRESENT, AND TO COME.
By W. BRIDGES ADAMS. 1 vol. post 8vo. 10s. 6d.

———— **(EDWIN) — GEOGRAPHY CLASSIFIED:**
a Systematic Manual of Mathematical, Physical, and Political Geography, with Geographical,
Etymological, and Historical Notes. For the use of Teachers and Upper Forms in Schools.
By EDWIN ADAMS, F.R.G.S., Author of 'The Geographical Word Expositor and Dictionary." Crown 8vo. cloth. 7s. 6d.'

AINSWORTH—THE LORD MAYOR OF LONDON,
By WILLIAM HARRISON AINSWORTH. 3 vols. post 8vo. 1l. 11s. 6d.

———————— **THE CONSTABLE OF THE TOWER,**
Third Edition. 1 vol. crown 8vo. 5s.

ALL THE YEAR ROUND.
Conducted by CHARLES DICKENS. Vols. I. to VIII., handsomely bound. 5s. 6d. each.

ALISON — THE PHILOSOPHY AND HISTORY OF
CIVILIZATION. By ALEXANDER ALISON. Demy 8vo. cloth. 14s.

ATLASES AND MAPS,
FOR STUDENTS AND TRAVELLERS; with Railways and Telegraphs, accurately
laid down.

    SHARPE'S ATLAS. Constructed upon a System of Scale and Proportion,
from the more recent Authorities. With a Copious Index. Fifty-four Maps. Large folio,
half morocco, plain, 36s.; coloured, 42s.

    SHARPE'S STUDENT'S ATLAS. With a Copious Index. Twenty-six
Coloured Maps, selected from the above. Folio, half-bound. 21s.

    LOWRY'S TABLE ATLAS. With a Copious Index. One Hundred
Coloured Maps. Large 4to. half-bound. 12s.

ATLASES AND MAPS—*continued.*

SIDNEY HALL'S TRAVELLING ATLAS OF THE ENGLISH COUNTIES, containing Fifty Maps, bound in a portable 8vo. Volume, in roan tuck. 10s. 6d.

SIDNEY HALL'S ATLAS OF THE ENGLISH COUNTIES, Enlarged Series, with General Maps of Great Britain, Scotland, Ireland, and Wales. 4to. half-bound, 24s., and folio, half-bound, 24s.

SIDNEY HALL'S MAPS OF ENGLISH COUNTIES, Enlarged Series, with all the Railways and Country Seats. Coloured, in neat wrapper, price 6d. each.

SHARPE'S TRAVELLING MAP OF ENGLAND AND WALES, with Railways and Electric Telegraph laid down to the present time. Coloured and mounted, in cloth case, 2s. 6d.

SHARPE'S TRAVELLING MAP OF SCOTLAND, with Railways and Electric Telegraph laid down to the present time. Coloured and mounted, in cloth case, 1s. 6d.

SHARPE'S TRAVELLING MAP OF IRELAND, with Railways and Electric Telegraph laid down to the present time. Coloured and mounted, in cloth case, 1s. 6d.

AUSTIN—TWO LETTERS ON GIRLS' SCHOOLS,
and on the Training of Working Women. By Mrs. AUSTIN. Post 8vo. sewed. 1s.

BAGEHOT—ESTIMATES OF SOME ENGLISHMEN
AND SCOTCHMEN: A Series of Essays contributed principally to the 'National Review.' By WALTER BAGEHOT. Demy 8vo. cloth. 14s.

BARHAM—PHILADELPHIA; OR, THE CLAIMS OF
HUMANITY: A PLEA FOR SOCIAL AND RELIGIOUS REFORM. By THOMAS FOSTER BARHAM, M.B. Cantab. Post 8vo. cloth. 6s. 6d.

BARRY CORNWALL—ENGLISH SONGS, AND
OTHER POEMS. By BARRY CORNWALL. New Edition, 24mo. sewed. 2s. 6d.

BEEVER (REV. W. HOLT)—NOTES ON FIELDS
AND CATTLE, from the Diary of an Amateur Farmer. With Illustrations. 1 vol. post 8vo. 8s. 6d.

BELLEW—LIFE IN CHRIST, AND CHRIST IN
LIFE. A NEW VOLUME OF SERMONS. By the Rev. J. M. BELLEW. 8vo. cloth. 12s

BLAGDEN (ISABELLA)—THE COST OF A SECRET.
By the Author of 'Agnes Tremorne.' 3 vols. post 8vo. cloth. 31s. 6d.

BLANC—HISTORICAL REVELATIONS.
Inscribed to Lord Normanby. By LOUIS BLANC. Post 8vo. cloth. 10s. 6d.

BLANCHARD (SIDNEY LAMAN) — THE GANGES
AND THE SEINE: Scenes on the Banks of Both. By SIDNEY LAMAN BLANCHARD. 2 vols. post 8vo. cloth. 18s.

BORDER LANDS OF SPAIN AND FRANCE (THE);
WITH AN ACCOUNT OF A VISIT TO THE REPUBLIC OF ANDORRE. Post 8vo. cloth. 10s. 6d.

BOURNE—A MEMOIR OF SIR PHILIP SIDNEY.
By H. H. R. FOX BOURNE. 1 vol. demy 8vo. 15s.

BRADLEY—ELEMENTS OF GEOMETRICAL DRAW-
ING, OR PRACTICAL GEOMETRY, PLANE AND SOLID. By THOMAS BRADLEY, of the Royal Military College, Woolwich. In Two Parts. Illustrated by Sixty Plates engraved by J. W. Lowry. Oblong folio, cloth. Each 16s.

BROWNE—HUNTING BITS.
By H. K. BROWNE (Phiz). Twelve Coloured Illustrations. Oblong folio, half bound 1l. 1s.

————————————————————. Proofs. 1l. 11s. 6d.

BROWNING (E. B.) — POETICAL WORKS.
By ELIZABETH BARRETT BROWNING. Fifth Edition, with Corrections and Additions. Three vols. fcap. cloth. 18s.

———————————————— AURORA LEIGH; A POEM.
IN NINE BOOKS. By ELIZABETH BARRETT BROWNING. Fifth Edition, with Portrait of Mrs. Browning. One vol. fcap. cloth. 7s.

———————————————— LAST POEMS.
Second Edition. 1 vol. crown 8vo. 6s.

———————————————— POEMS BEFORE CONGRESS.
By ELIZABETH BARRETT BROWNING. Crown 8vo. cloth. 4s.

———————————————— THE GREEK CHRISTIAN
POETS, AND THE ENGLISH POETS. By ELIZABETH BARRETT BROWNING. Fcap. 8vo. cloth. 5s.

BROWNING (ROBERT) — POETICAL WORKS.
By ROBERT BROWNING. A New Edition, with numerous Alterations and Additions. Three vols. fcap. cloth.   [In the press.

———————————————— A SELECTION FROM THE
POEMS OF ROBERT BROWNING. Fcap. 8vo. cloth. 6s.

———————————————— MEN AND WOMEN.
BY ROBERT BROWNING. In two vols. fcap. 8vo. cloth. 12s.

———————————————— CHRISTMAS EVE AND
EASTER DAY. A POEM. By ROBERT BROWNING. Fcap. 8vo. cloth. 6s.

A 3

BURCHETT — LINEAR PERSPECTIVE.

For the Use of Schools of Art. By R. BURCHETT, Head Master of the Training Schools for Art Masters of the Science and Art Department. Fifth Edition. Post 8vo. cloth, with Illustrations. 7s.

—————————— PRACTICAL GEOMETRY.

THE COURSE OF CONSTRUCTION OF PLANE GEOMETRICAL FIGURES. By R. BURCHETT. With 137 Diagrams. Fifth Edition. Post 8vo. cloth. 5s.

—————————— DEFINITIONS OF GEOMETRY.

24mo. sewed. 5d.

BUTT — THE HISTORY OF ITALY FROM THE

ABDICATION OF NAPOLEON I. With Introductory References to that of Earlier Times. Two vols. 8vo. cloth. 36s.

MR. THOMAS CARLYLE'S WORKS.

UNIFORM EDITION.

Handsomely printed in Crown Octavo, price Six Shillings per Volume.

THE FRENCH REVOLUTION: A HISTORY. In 2 Volumes. 12s.

OLIVER CROMWELL'S LETTERS AND SPEECHES. With Elucidations and Connecting Narrative. In 3 Volumes. 18s.

LIFE OF JOHN STERLING.
LIFE OF SCHILLER. } One Vol. 6s.

CRITICAL AND MISCELLANEOUS ESSAYS. In 4 Volumes. 24s.

SARTOR RESARTUS.
HERO WORSHIP. } One Volume. 6s.

LATTER-DAY PAMPHLETS. One Volume. 6s.

CHARTISM.
PAST AND PRESENT. } One Volume. 6s.

TRANSLATIONS OF GERMAN ROMANCE. One Volume. 6s.

WILHELM MEISTER. By GÖTHE. A Translation. In 2 Volumes. 12s.

CARLYLE — HISTORY OF FRIEDRICH THE SECOND,

called FREDERICK THE GREAT. By THOMAS CARLYLE. With Portraits and Maps. Third Edition. Vols. I. and II., Third Edition, demy 8vo. cloth, 40s. Vol. III., demy 8vo. cloth. 20s. Vol. IV. in the Press.

CHAPMAN AND HALL'S
SELECT LIBRARY OF FICTION.

PRICE TWO SHILLINGS EACH NOVEL.

MARY BARTON : a Tale of Manchester Life.

RUTH. A Novel. By the Author of 'Mary Barton.'

CRANFORD. By the Author of 'Mary Barton.'

LIZZIE LEIGH; and other Tales. By the Author of 'Mary Barton.'

THE HEAD OF THE FAMILY. A Novel.

AGATHA'S HUSBAND. By the Author of 'John Halifax, Gentleman.'

OLIVE. A Novel. By the Author of 'The Head of the Family.'

THE OGILVIES. A Novel. By the Author of 'The Head of the Family.'

ALTON LOCKE : Tailor and Poet. By the Rev. CHARLES KINGSLEY. With a new Preface, addressed to the Working Men of Great Britain.

THE BACHELOR OF THE ALBANY. By M. W. SAVAGE.

MY UNCLE THE CURATE. A Novel. By M. W. SAVAGE.

THE HALF SISTERS. A Tale. By Miss JEWSBURY.

THE BLITHEDALE ROMANCE. By NATHANIEL HAWTHORNE.

PRICE ONE SHILLING EACH NOVEL.

THE WHITEBOY. A Story of Ireland in 1822. By Mrs. S. C. HALL.

EUSTACE CONYERS. By JAMES HANNAY.

MARETIMO : A Story of Adventure. By BAYLE ST. JOHN.

MELINCOURT. By the Author of 'Headlong Hall.'

THE FALCON FAMILY; or, Young Ireland. A Satirical Novel. By M. W. SAVAGE.

*** Other Popular Novels will be issued in this Series.*

Notices of the Press.

'The Fictions published by this Firm in their "Select Library" have all been of a high character.'—*Press.*

'Who would be satisfied with the much-thumbed "Library Book," when he can procure, in one handsome volume, a celebrated Work of Fiction now offered by Messrs. Chapman and Hall at the low price of Two Shillings?'—*Britannia.*

'Capital Novels, well worth the price asked for them.'—*Guardian.*

A 4

CHAPMAN AND HALL'S
STANDARD EDITIONS OF POPULAR AUTHORS.

ANTHONY TROLLOPE'S WEST INDIES AND THE SPANISH MAIN. Fifth Edition. 5s.

ANTHONY TROLLOPE'S CASTLE RICHMOND. A Novel. Fourth Edition. 5s.

ANTHONY TROLLOPE'S DOCTOR THORNE. A Novel. Seventh Edition. 5s.

ANTHONY TROLLOPE'S BERTRAMS. A Novel. Sixth Edition. 5s.

ANTHONY TROLLOPE'S KELLYS AND THE O'KELLYS. Fourth Edition. 5s.

ANTHONY TROLLOPE'S MACDERMOTS OF BALLYCLORAN. Fifth Edition. 5s.

T. A. TROLLOPE'S LA BEATA (Third Edition); and a TUSCAN ROMEO AND JULIET. 5s.

J. CORDY JEAFFRESON'S OLIVE BLAKE'S GOOD WORK. Third Edition. 5s.

MARKET HARBOROUGH (Fifth Edition); and INSIDE THE BAR. By the Author of 'Digby Grand.' 5s.

TILBURY NOGO. By the Author of 'Digby Grand.' Third Edition. 5s.

W. M. THACKERAY'S IRISH SKETCH-BOOK. With Illustrations by the Author. Fourth Edition. Crown 8vo. 5s.   [*In May.*

ALBERT SMITH'S WILD OATS AND DEAD LEAVES. Second Edition. Crown 8vo. 5s.

MRS. GASKELL'S NORTH AND SOUTH. Fourth Edition. 5s.

G. A. SALA'S GASLIGHT AND DAYLIGHT; with some London Scenes they Shine upon. Second Edition. 5s.

WILLIAM HARRISON AINSWORTH'S CONSTABLE OF THE TOWER. Third Edition. 5s.

WILLIAM HARRISON AINSWORTH'S LORD MAYOR OF LONDON. Second Edition. 5s.

W. H. WILLS' OLD LEAVES GATHERED FROM 'HOUSE- HOLD WORDS.' 5s.

ROBERT-HOUDIN'S MEMOIRS: Ambassador, Author, and Conjuror. Written by HIMSELF. Third Edition. 5s.

MISS MULOCK'S HEAD OF THE FAMILY. Sixth Edition. 5s.

MISS ANNA DRURY'S MISREPRESENTATION. Third Edition. 5s.

ESQUIROS—THE ENGLISH AT HOME. Second Series.
By ALPHONSE ESQUIROS. Translated by LASCELLES WRAXALL. 1 vol. post 8vo.
10s. 6d.

———————————THE DUTCH AT HOME.
By ALPHONSE ESQUIROS. Translated by LASCELLES WRAXALL. 2 vols. post
8vo. 18s.
New Edition, in one vol.   [In the press.

FAIRHOLT—UP THE NILE AND HOME AGAIN.
A Handbook for Travellers, and a Travel-Book for the Library. By F. W. FAIRHOLT,
F.S.A. With 100 Illustrations from Original Sketches by the Author. 1 vol. post 8vo. 16s.

FINLAISON — NEW GOVERNMENT SUCCESSION-
DUTY TABLES. For the Use of Successors to Property, their Solicitors and Agents, and
others concerned in the Payment of the Duties Levied on all Successions, under Authority
of the present Statute, 16 & 17 Victoria, cap. 51. By ALEXANDER GLEN FINLAISON.
Post 8vo. cloth. 5s. New Edition.   [In the press.

FOSTER—HISTORY OF ENGLAND FOR SCHOOLS
AND FAMILIES. By A. F. FOSTER. With numerous Illustrations. Post 8vo. cloth. 6s.

——————— ELEMENTS OF GEOGRAPHY.
By A. F. FOSTER. Post cloth. 5s.

FORSTER (JOHN) — OLIVER GOLDSMITH.
A Biography. By JOHN FORSTER. With Forty Illustrations. New Edition. Post 8o.
cloth. 7s. 6d.

FRANCATELLI—ROYAL CONFECTIONER.
By C. E. FRANCATELLI. With numerous Coloured Illustrations. Post 8vo. cloth. 12s.

FREYTAG — PICTURES FROM GERMAN LIFE, IN
THE FIFTEENTH, SIXTEENTH, AND SEVENTEENTH CENTURIES. By HERR
FREYTAG, Author of 'Debit and Credit.' Translated by Mrs. MALCOLM. 1l. 1s.
Also, in May, the SECOND PORTION, including the EIGHTEENTH and NINE-
TEENTH CENTURIES. In 2 vols. post 8vo.

FROM HAY-TIME TO HOPPING.
By the Author of 'Our Farm of Four Acres.' Second edition, small 8vo. cloth. 5s.

GARDEN THAT PAID THE RENT (THE).
Fourth edition, post 8vo. boards. 2s.

GASKELL.—CRANFORD—MARY BARTON—RUTH—
LIZZIE LEIGH. By Mrs. GASKELL. Post 8vo. boards. Price 2s. each.

——————— NORTH AND SOUTH.
Fourth and cheaper edition. Crown 8vo. cloth. 5s.

GASKELL — MOORLAND COTTAGE.
With Illustrations by BIRKET FOSTER. Fcap. 8vo. cloth. 2s. 6d.

GERMAN LOVE.
FROM THE PAPERS OF AN ALIEN. Translated by SUSANNA WINKWORTH,
with the sanction of the Author. Fcap. cloth. 4s. 6d.

GRATTAN (THOMAS COLLEY.) — BEATEN PATHS,
AND THOSE WHO TROD THEM. Second Edition. 2 vols. post 8vo. 16s.

HARVEY (MRS.) — OUR CRUISE IN THE CLAY-
MORE; WITH A VISIT TO DAMASCUS AND THE LEBANON. By MRS.
HARVEY, of Ickwell-Bury. In post 8vo. cloth, with Illustrations. Price 10s. 6d,

HAWKINS — A COMPARATIVE VIEW OF THE
ANIMAL AND HUMAN FRAME. By B. WATERHOUSE HAWKINS, F.L.S., F.G.S.,
with Ten Illustrations from Nature by the Author. Folio, cloth. 12s.

HAXTHAUSEN—THE RUSSIAN EMPIRE.
ITS PEOPLE, INSTITUTIONS, AND RESOURCES. By Baron VON HAXTHAUSEN,
Author of 'Transcaucasia,' &c. Translated and issued under the immediate sanction of
the Author. In 2 vols. 8vo. cloth. 28s.

——————————TRANSCAUCASIA.
Sketches of the Nations and Races between the Black Sea and the Caspian. By Baron
VON HAXTHAUSEN. With Eight Coloured Illustrations by GRAEB. 8vo. cloth. 18s.

——————————THE TRIBES OF THE CAUCASUS;
WITH AN ACCOUNT OF SCHAMYL AND THE MURIDS. By BARON VON
HAXTHAUSEN. Post 8vo. cloth. 6s.

HEATON—THE THRESHOLD OF CHEMISTRY;
An Experimental Introduction to the Science. By CHARLES HEATON. With numerous Illustrations. Post 8vo. cloth. 4s.

HEINRICH HEINE'S BOOK OF SONGS.
A Translation. By JOHN E. WALLIS. Crown 8vo. cloth. 9s.

HENSLOW—ILLUSTRATIONS TO BE EMPLOYED
IN THE PRACTICAL LESSONS ON BOTANY. Adapted to all classes. Prepared for
the South Kensington Museum. By the Rev. PROFESSOR HENSLOW. With Illustrations. Post 8vo. 6d.

HOUDIN (ROBERT) — THE SHARPER DECTECTED
AND EXPOSED. By ROBERT HOUDIN, Author of 'Memoirs of Robert Houdin.'
With Illustrations. Post 8vo. cloth. 6s.

HOUSEHOLD WORDS.
Conducted by CHARLES DICKENS. 19 vols. royal 8vo. cloth. 5s. 6d. each. (All the back Numbers and Parts may now be had.)

HOUSEHOLD WORDS — CHRISTMAS STORIES
FROM. Royal 8vo. cloth. 2s. 6d.

INDUSTRIAL AND SOCIAL POSITION OF WOMEN,
IN THE MIDDLE AND LOWER RANKS. Post 8vo. cloth. 10s. 6d.

JEAFFRESON (JOHN CORDY) — OLIVE BLAKE'S
GOOD WORK. Third Edition. 1 vol. crown. 5s.

JERVIS—THE RIFLE-MUSKET.
A Practical Treatise on the Enfield-Prichett Rifle, recently adopted in the British Service. By CAPTAIN JERVIS WHITE JERVIS, M.P., Royal Artillery, Author of the 'Manual of Field Operations.' Second and Cheaper Edition, with Additions. Post 8vo. cloth. 2s.

————OUR ENGINES OF WAR, AND HOW WE
GOT TO MAKE THEM. By CAPTAIN JERVIS WHITE JERVIS, M.P., Royal Artillery. With many Illustrations. Post 8vo. cloth. 6s.

———— THE IONIAN ISLANDS · DURING THE
PRESENT CENTURY. By Captain WHYTE-JERVIS, M.P. Post 8vo. cloth. 3s. 6d.

JEWSBURY—THE HALF-SISTERS.
A Novel. By GERALDINE E. JEWSBURY. Cheap Edition. Post 8vo., boards. 2s.

KEIGHTLEY—THE LIFE, OPINIONS, AND WRIT-
INGS OF JOHN MILTON. With an Introduction to 'Paradise Lost.' By THOMAS KEIGHTLEY. Second Edition. Demy 8vo. cloth. 10s. 6d.

————THE POEMS OF JOHN MILTON.
WITH NOTES by THOMAS KEIGHTLEY. 2 vols. 8vo. cloth. 21s.

KELLY—LIFE IN VICTORIA IN 1853 AND IN 1858.
By WILLIAM KELLY. 2 vols. post 8vo., cloth. 21s.

KOHL (J. G.)—POPULAR HISTORY OF THE DIS-
COVERY OF AMERICA, FROM COLUMBUS TO FRANKLIN. Translated by MAJOR R. R. NOEL. 2 vols. post 8vo. 16s.

————KITCHI-GAMI:
WANDERINGS ROUND LAKE SUPERIOR. By J. G. KOHL. With Woodcuts. 8vo. cloth. 13s.

LEAVES FROM THE DIARY OF AN OFFICER OF
THE GUARDS DURING THE PENINSULAR WAR. By LIEUT.-COL. STEPNEY COWELL STEPNEY, K.H., late Coldstream Guards. Fcap. cloth. 5s.

LENNARD—TALES FROM MOLIÈRE'S PLAYS.
By DACRE BARRETT LENNARD. Post 8vo. cloth. 10s. 6d.

MR. CHARLES LEVER'S WORKS.
LIBRARY EDITION.
IN DEMY OCTAVO, ILLUSTRATED BY PHIZ.

BARRINGTON.   Demy 8vo. cloth.   With 26 Illustrations. 14s.

ONE OF THEM.   Demy 8vo., cloth. With 30 Illustrations. 7s.

DAVENPORT DUNN; A Man of Our Day.   2 Vols., demy 8vo., cloth. With 44 Illustrations. 14s.

THE MARTINS OF CRO' MARTIN. 2 Vols. With 40 Illustrations. 14s.

HARRY LORREQUER.   1 Vol.   With 22 Illustrations. 7s.

CHARLES O'MALLEY, THE IRISH DRAGOON. 2 Vols. With 44 Illustrations. 14s.

JACK HINTON, THE GUARDSMAN. 1 Vol. With 26 Illustrations. 7s.

TOM BURKE OF 'OURS.' 2 Vols. With 44 Illustrations. 14s.

THE O'DONOGHUE: A Tale of Ireland Fifty Years Ago. 1 Vol. With 26 Illustrations. 7s.

THE KNIGHT OF GWYNNE. 2 Vols. With 40 Illustrations. 14s.

ROLAND CASHEL.   2 Vols.   With 40 Illustrations.   14s.

THE DALTONS; OR, Three Roads in Life. 2 Vols. With 44 Illustrations. 14s.

THE DODD FAMILY ABROAD. 2 Vols. With 40 Illustrations. 14s.

CHEAP AND UNIFORM EDITION,
WITH ILLUSTRATIONS BY H. K. BROWNE.
This Edition is handsomely printed in Crown Octavo. Each Volume contains
EIGHT ENGRAVINGS BY H. K. BROWNE.
Bound in Cloth. Price 4s.

JACK HINTON. 4s.

TOM BURKE OF 'OURS.' In 2 Vols. 8s.

HARRY LORREQUER. 4s.

CHARLES O'MALLEY, THE IRISH DRAGOON. In 2 Vols. 8s.

THE O'DONOGHUE. 4s.

THE KNIGHT OF GWYNNE. In 2 Vols. 8s.

ROLAND CASHEL. In 2 Vols. 8s.

THE DALTONS. In 2 Vols. 8s.

THE DODD FAMILY ABROAD. In 2 Vols. 8s.

MARTINS OF CRO' MARTIN. In 2 Vols. 8s.

FORTUNES OF GLENCOE. In 1 Vol. 4s.

ONE OF THEM. In 1 Vol. 4s.

DAVENPORT DUNN. In 2 Vols. 8s.

LEVER'S (CHARLES) WORKS.　CHEAP EDITION.

JACK HINTON.　2s.

CHARLES O'MALLEY.　2 vols.　4s.

THE DALTONS.　2 vols.　4s.

HARRY LORREQUER.　2s.

THE KNIGHT OF GWYNNE.　2 vols.　4s.

DODD FAMILY ABROAD.　2 vols.　4s.

THE O'DONOGHUE.　2s.

ROLAND CASHEL.　2 vols.　4s.

TOM BURKE.　2 vols.　4s.

DAVENPORT DUNN.　2 vols.　4s.

LIFE IN THE SOUTH FROM THE COMMENCE-

MENT OF THE WAR.　By a Blockaded British Subject.　Being a Social History of those who took part in the Battles, from a personal accquaintance with them in their own homes.　2 vols. post 8vo. cloth.　21s.

LOWRY'S ATLAS.

With a Copious Index.　100 Coloured Maps.　Large 4to., half-bound.　12s.

A New Series of Maps, in large 4to., price One Penny each Map plain, and Two Pence with the Boundaries coloured, completed in 100 Maps, any of which can be purchased separately, plain 1d., coloured 2d.

LIST OF THE MAPS.

Sheet.		Sheet.	
1, 2.	World in Hemispheres—2 Maps.	54, 55.	Turkey in Asia and Western Persia—2 Maps.
3, 4.	World on Mercator's Projection—2 Maps.	56.	Eastern Persia.
5.	Europe.	57, 58.	Syria and Arabia Petræa—2 Maps.
6.	British Isles.	59, 60.	China and Indian Seas—2 Maps.
7, 8.	England and Wales—2 Maps.	61.	Australia and New Zealand—General Map.
9.	Scotland—General.		
10.	Ireland—General.	62, 63.	Australia—2 Maps.
11.	France, in Provinces.	64 to 66.	New South Wales—3 Maps.
12 to 15.	France in Departments—4 Maps.	67.	Victoria or Port Phillip District.'
16.	Holland and Belgium.	68.	New Zealand.
17.	Spain and Portugal—General.	69, 70.	Polynesia—2 Maps.
18 to 21.	Spain and Portugal—4 Maps.	71, 72.	Africa—2 Maps.
22.	Italy—General.	73 to 75.	Egypt, Nubia, Abyssinia, and Red Sea—3 Maps.
23 to 26.	Italy—4 Maps.		
27.	Prussia and German States.	76, 77.	North Africa—comprising Morocco, Algiers, and Tunis—2 Maps.
28 to 31.	Germany and Switzerland—4 Maps.		
32.	Austrian Empire.	78 to 80.	West Africa—comprising Senegambia, Liberia, Soudan, and Guinea—3 Maps.
33, 34.	Hungary and Transylvania—2 Maps.		
35.	Turkey in Europe and Greece.	81, 82.	Southern Africa—2 Maps.
36.	Bosphorus and Dardanelles.	83.	British North America.
37.	Greece and the Ionian Islands.	84.	Arctic Regions.
38, 39.	Sweden and Norway—2 Maps.	85, 86.	Canada, New Brunswick, and Nova Scotia—2 Maps.
40.	Denmark.		
41.	Russia in Europe.	87.	North America—General.
42.	Asia, North.	88, 89.	United States—2 Maps—General.
43, 44.	Asia, South, and Indian Seas—2 Maps.	90 to 93.	United States—4 Maps.
		94.	Mexico.
45.	India—General.	95.	West Indies and Central America.
46 to 52.	India—7 Maps.	96.	South America—General.
53.	Persia and Tartary.	97 to 100.	South America—4 Maps.

LYTTON—MONEY.
A Comedy, in Five Acts. By Sir EDWARD BULWER LYTTON. 8vo. sewed. 2s. 6d.

———— NOT SO BAD AS WE SEEM;
OR, MANY SIDES TO A CHARACTER. A Comedy, in Five Acts. By Sir EDWARD BULWER LYTTON. 8vo. sewed. 2s. 6d.

———— RICHELIEU; OR, THE CONSPIRACY.
A Play, in Five Acts. By Sir EDWARD BULWER LYTTON. 8vo. sewed. 2s. 6d.

———— THE LADY OF LYONS;
OR, LOVE AND PRIDE. A Play, in Five Acts. By Sir EDWARD BULWER LYTTON. 8vo. sewed. 2s. 6d.

M'CULLAGH — INDUSTRIAL HISTORY OF FREE
NATIONS. Considered in Relation to their Domestic Institutions and External Policy. By W. TORRENS M'CULLAGH. 2 vols. 8vo. cloth. 24s.

————USE AND STUDY OF HISTORY.
Being the Substance of a Course of Lectures delivered in Dublin. By W. TORRENS M'CULLAGH. Second edition, 8vo. cloth. 10s. 6d.

MACKNIGHT—HISTORY OF THE LIFE AND TIMES
OF EDMUND BURKE. By THOMAS MACKNIGHT, Author of 'The Right Hon. B. Disraeli, M.P., a Literary and Political Biography;' and 'Thirty Years of Foreign Policy, a History of the Secretaryships of the Earl of Aberdeen and Viscount Palmerston.' 3 vols. demy 8vo. cloth, price 50s.

———— (THOMAS) — THE LIFE OF LORD
BOLINGBROKE, Secretary of State in the reign of Queen Anne. By THOMAS MAC-KNIGHT. Demy 8vo. cloth. 18s.

MACREADY—LEAVES FROM THE OLIVE MOUNT.
Poems. By CATHERINE FRANCES B. MACREADY. Fcap. 8vo. cloth. 5s.

MALLET—COTTON:
The Chemical, Geological, and Meteorological Conditions involved in its Successful Cultivation. With an Account of the Actual Conditions and Practice of Culture in the Southern or Cotton States of North America. By Dr. JOHN WILLIAM MALLET, Ph. D. University of Gottingen, A.B. Trin. Coll. Dublin, Professor of Chemistry in the University of Alabama, Analytical Chemist of the State Geological Survey, and Chemical Professor to the State School of Medicine, Mobile. 1 vol. post 8vo. With Illustrations. 7s. 6d.

———— (ROBERT) — THE FIRST PRINCIPLES OF
OBSERVATIONAL SEISMOLOGY: as developed in the Report to the Royal Society of London, of the Expedition made by command of the Society into the interior of the kingdom of Naples, to investigate the circumstances of the great Neapolitan Earthquake of December, 1857. By ROBERT MALLET, C.E., F.R.S., F.G.S., M.R.I.A., &c. &c. Published by the Authority and with the Aid of the Royal Society of London. In 2 vols. royal 8vo., with numerous Illustrations in Lithography and Wood, and Maps. £3. 3s.

MARIOTTI—ITALY IN 1848.
By L. MARIOTTI. 8vo. cloth. 12s.

MARKET HARBOROUGH; OR, HOW MR. SAWYER
WENT TO THE SHIRES. Fifth Edition. And INSIDE THE BAR, now first published. By the Author of 'Digby Grand.' 5s.

MARSHALL—POPULATION & TRADE IN FRANCE,
1861-62. By FREDERICK MARSHALL. 1 vol. post 8vo. 8s.

MAZZINI (JOSEPH)—THE DUTIES OF MAN.
By JOSEPH MAZZINI. Post 8vo. 7s.

MELINCOURT;
OR, SIR ORAN HAUT-TON By the Author of 'Headlong Hall,' &c. Cheap Edition. Post 8vo. boards. 1s.

MEMOIRS OF ROBERT-HOUDIN,
Ambassador, Author, and Conjuror. Written by Himself. Third and cheaper Edition. crown 8vo. cloth. 5s.

MENZIES—EARLY ANCIENT HISTORY;
Or, The Ante-Greek Period as it appears to us since the most recent Discoveries in Egypt and Assyria. With References to Wilkinson, Layard, and other authorities. Intended for popular use. By HENRY MENZIES. 1 vol. post 8vo. 4s. 6d.

MEREDITH (L. A.)—OVER THE STRAITS.
By LOUISA ANNE MEREDITH. With Illustrations. Post 8vo. cloth. 9s.

MEREDITH (OWEN)—LUCILE. A POEM.
By OWEN MEREDITH. Crown 8vo. cloth. 12s.

—————————— SERBSKI PESME;
OR, NATIONAL SONGS OF SERVIA. By OWEN MEREDITH. Fcap. cloth. 4s.

—————————— THE WANDERER.
A Poem. By the Author of 'Clytemnestra,' &c. Second edition, foolscap 8vo. cloth. 9s. 6d.

MEREDITH (GEORGE)—THE SHAVING OF SHAG-
PAT. An Arabian Entertainment. By GEORGE MEREDITH. Post 8vo. cloth. 10s. 6d.

—————————— THE ORDEAL OF RICHARD
FEVEREL. By GEORGE MEREDITH. 3 vols. post 8vo. cloth. 31s. 6d.

—————————— MODERN LOVE:
And Poems of the English Roadside. 1 vol. fcap. 8vo. 6s.

MICHIELS—SECRET HISTORY OF THE AUSTRIAN
GOVERNMENT, AND OF ITS SYSTEMATIC PERSECUTIONS OF PROTESTANTS. Compiled from official documents. By ALFRED MICHIELS. Post 8vo. cloth. 10s. 6d.

MONEY —TWELVE MONTHS WITH THE BASHI-
BAZOUKS. By EDWARD MONEY. With Coloured Illustrations. Post 8vo. cloth. 7s

MORGAN—THE MIND OF SHAKSPERE, AS EX-
HIBITED IN HIS WORKS. By the Rev. A. A. MORGAN, M.A. Second edition, foolscap 8vo. cloth. 6s.

MORISON (J. COTTER) — LIFE AND TIMES OF
ST. BERNARD, ABBOT OF CLAIRVAUX. Demy 8vo. cloth. 14s.

MORLEY—MEMOIRS OF BARTHOLOMEW FAIR.
By HENRY MORLEY. With Eighty Illustrations. Demy 8vo. cloth. 21s.

————————THE LIFE OF HENRY CORNELIUS
AGRIPPA VON NETTESHEIM, Doctor and Knight, commonly known as a Magician. By HENRY MORLEY. In 2 vols. post 8vo. cloth. 18s.

————————JEROME CARDAN.
A BIOGRAPHY. By HENRY MORLEY. Two vols. post 8vo. cloth. 18s.

———————— THE LIFE OF BERNARD PALISSY, OF
SAINTES. His Labours and Discoveries in Arts and Science. By HENRY MORLEY. Post 8vo. cloth. Price 12s. Second and cheaper Edition.

————————HOW TO MAKE HOME UNHEALTHY.
By HENRY MORLEY. Reprinted from the 'Examiner.' Second edition, small 8vo. stiff wrapper. 1s.

———————— A DEFENCE OF IGNORANCE.
By HENRY MORLEY. Small 8vo. cloth. 3s.

MULOCK—THE HEAD OF THE FAMILY.
By Miss MULOCK. Sixth edition, crown 8vo. cloth, 5s. Cheap edition, post 8vo. boards. 2s.

————————OLIVE; A NOVEL.
By Miss MULOCK. Cheap edition, post 8vo. boards. 2s.

————————THE OGILVIES; A NOVEL.
By Miss MULOCK. Cheap edition, post 8vo. boards. 2s.

————————AGATHA'S HUSBAND.
By Miss MULOCK. Cheap edition, post 8vo. boards. 2s.

MUSHET—BOOK OF SYMBOLS.
A Series of Seventy-five Short Essays on Morals, Religion, and Philosophy. Each Essay Illustrating an Ancient Symbol or Modern Precept. By ROBERT MUSHET. Second edition, post 8vo. cloth. 6s.

NORTH AND SOUTH.
By the White Republican of Fraser's Magazine. Post 8vo. cloth. 9s.

NORTON—CHILD OF THE ISLANDS; A POEM.
By the Hon. Mrs. NORTON. Second edition, square 8vo. cloth. 6s.

OUR FARM OF FOUR ACRES, AND THE MONEY
WE MADE BY IT. Eighteenth edition, small post 8vo. boards. 1s.

PACKET (A) OF SEEDS SAVED BY AN OLD GAR-
DENER. Second Edition, Enlarged. Crown 8vo. bds. 1s. 6d.

PEACOCK—GL' INGANNATI THE DECEIVED.
A Comedy. By T. L. PEACOCK. Fcap. cloth. 3s. 6d.

PETO (SIR S. MORTON, BART., M.P.)—TAXATION:
Its Levy and Expenditure Past and Future; being an Inquiry into our Financial Policy.
By Sir S. MORTON PETO, Bart, M.P. for Finsbury. Demy 8vo. cloth. 10s. 6d.

RAMBLES AND RECOLLECTIONS OF A FLY-
FISHER. Illustrated. With an Appendix, containing ample Instructions to the Novice,
inclusive of Fly-making, and a List of really useful Flies. By CLERICUS. With Eight
Illustrations. Post 8vo. cloth. 7s.

RÉCAMIER, MADAME, with a Sketch of the History of
Society in France. By Madame M——. 1 vol. post 8vo. 9s.

REDGRAVE—A MANUAL AND CATECHISM ON
COLOUR. By RICHARD REDGRAVE, R.A. 24mo. cloth. 9d.

RICHMOND—A MEMOIR OF THE LATE DUKE OF
RICHMOND. With a Portrait. 1 vol. demy 8vo. 15s.

RIDGE—HEALTH AND DISEASE, THEIR LAWS;
WITH PLAIN PRACTICAL PRESCRIPTIONS FOR THE PEOPLE. By BENJAMIN
RIDGE, M.D., F.R.C.S. Second Edition. Post 8vo., cloth. 12s.

———— OURSELVES, OUR FOOD, AND OUR
HYSIC. By Dr. BENJAMIN RIDGE. In fcap. 8vo. cloth. Third Edition. Price 1s. 6d.

ROBERT MORNAY.
By MAX FERRER. Post 8vo., cloth. 9s.

ROBINSON — THE ITALIAN SCULPTURE COLLEC-
TIONS OF THE SOUTH KENSINGTON MUSEUM. A Descriptive Catalogue, comprising an Account of the Acquisitions from the Gigli and Campana Collections. Illustrated
with 20 Engravings. By J. C. ROBINSON, F.S.A., &c., Superintendent of the Art Collections of the South Kensington Museum. By Authority of the Committee of Council on
Education. In a handsome royal 8vo. volume. 7s. 6d.

———— (J. C.)—SOUTH KENSINGTON MUSEUM.
Italian Sculptures of the Middle Ages and Period of the Revival of Art. A Series of 50
Photographs of Works in the above Section of the Museum, Selected and Arranged by
J. C. ROBINSON, F.S.A. The Photographs executed by C. THURSTON THOMPSON. In
one large handsome folio volume. £6. 6s. Published by Authority of the Science and
Art Department of the Committee of Council on Education.

RODENBERG—THE ISLAND OF THE SAINTS, A
PILGRIMAGE THROUGH IRELAND. By JULIUS RODENBERG. Translated by
LASCELLES WRAXALL. Post 8vo., cloth. 9s.

ROMAN CANDLES.
Post 8vo., cloth. 8s.

ROSCOE—POEMS, TRAGEDIES, AND ESSAYS.
By WILLIAM CALDWELL ROSCOE. Edited, with a Prefatory Memoir, by his
brother-in-law, RICHARD HOLT HUTTON. Two vols. crown 8vo., cloth. 21s.

SALA—GASLIGHT AND DAYLIGHT, WITH SOME
LONDON SCENES THEY SHINE UPON. By GEORGE AUGUSTUS SALA. Crown
8vo., cloth. Second Edition. 5s.

ST. JOHN, BAYLE—THE SUBALPINE KINGDOM;
Or, EXPERIENCES AND STUDIES IN SAVOY, PIEDMONT, AND GENOA. By
BAYLE ST. JOHN. 2 vols. Post 8vo., cloth. 21s.

——————————————— **TWO YEARS' RESIDENCE IN**
A LEVANTINE FAMILY. By BAYLE ST. JOHN. Cheap Edition. Post 8vo.
boards. 1s.

——————————————— **MARETIMO;**
A STORY OF ADVENTURE. By BAYLE ST. JOHN. Reprinted from 'Chambers'
Journal.' Post 8vo., boards. 1s.

——————————————— **THE LOUVRE;**
Or, BIOGRAPHY OF A MUSEUM. By BAYLE ST JOHN. Post 8vo., cloth. 10s. 6d.

ST. JOHN, J. A.—THE EDUCATION OF THE PEOPLE;
By JAMES AUGUSTUS ST. JOHN, Author of 'Isis,' 'Life of Louis Napoleon,' &c.
Post 8vo., cloth. 8s. 6d. Dedicated to Sir John Pakington, M.P.

——————————————— **ISIS; AN EGYPTIAN PILGRIMAGE.**
By JAMES AUGUSTUS ST. JOHN. Second Edition. 2 vols., post 8vo., cloth. 12s.

——————————————— **THE NEMESIS OF POWER: Causes**
and Forms of Revolution. By JAMES AUGUSTUS ST. JOHN. Fcap. cloth. 5s.

——————————————— **PHILOSOPHY AT THE FOOT OF**
THE CROSS. By JAMES AUGUSTUS ST. JOHN. Fcap. cloth. 5s.

——————————————— **THE PREACHING OF CHRIST, ITS**
NATURE AND CONSEQUENCES. By JAMES AUGUSTUS ST. JOHN. Small 8vo.,
sewed. 1s. 6d.

SAVAGE—BACHELOR OF THE ALBANY. A Novel.
By M. W. SAVAGE. Cheap Edition. Post 8vo., boards. 2s.

——————————— **THE FALCON FAMILY; or, YOUNG IRE-**
LAND. A Satirical Novel. By M. W. SAVAGE. Cheap Edition. Post 8vo., boards. 1s.

SAVAGE—MY UNCLE THE CURATE.

By M. W. SAVAGE. Cheap Edition. Post 8vo., boards. 2s.

———— CLOVER COTTAGE; or, I CAN'T GET IN.

A Novelette. By the Author of 'The Falcon Family,' &c. With Illustrations. In fcap. 8vo., cloth. 5s.

SHARPE'S ATLAS:

Comprising Fifty-four Maps, constructed upon a System of Scale and Proportion from the most recent Authorities, and Engraved on Steel, by J. WILSON LOWRY. With a Copious Consulting Index. In a large folio volume. Half morocco, gilt back and edges, plain, 36s.; or with the maps coloured, 42s.

CONTENTS.

1. The World—Western Hemisphere.
2. The World—Eastern Hemisphere.
3. The World—Mercator's Projection.
4. Europe, with the Mediterranean.
5. Great Britain and Ireland.
6. England and Wales—Railway Map, North.
7. England and Wales—Railway Map, South.
8. Scotland.
9. Ireland.
10. France—Belgium—Switzerland.
11. Belgium and Holland.
12. Prussia, Holland, and German States.
13. Switzerland.
14. Austrian Empire.
15. Turkey and Greece.
16. Greece.
17. Italy.
18. Spain and Portugal.
19. Northern Sweden, and Frontier of Russia.
20. Denmark, Sweden, and Russia on the Baltic.
21. Western Russia, from the Baltic to the Euxine.
22. Russia on the Euxine.
23. Russia on the Caucasus.
24. Russia in Europe.
25. Northern Asia—Asiatic Russia.
26. South-West. Asia—Overland to India.
27. South-Eastern Asia — Birmah, China, and Japan.
28. Australia and New Zealand.
29. Egypt and Arabia Petræa.
30. Nubia and Abyssinia to Babel Mandeb Strait.
31. Asia Minor.
32. Syria and the Turkish Provinces on the Persian Gulf.
33. Western Persia.
34. Eastern Persia.
35. Affghanistan and the Punjab.
36. Beloochistan and Scinde.
37. Central India.
38. The Carnatic.
39. Bengal, &c.
40. India—General Map.
41. North Africa.
42. South Africa.
43. British North America.
44. Central America.
45. United States—General Map.
46. United States—North-East.
47. United States—South-East.
48. United States—South-West.
49. Jamaica, and Leeward and Windward Islands.
50. Mexico and Guatemala.
51. South America.
52. Columbian and Peruvian Republics, and Western Brazil.
53. La Plata, Chili, and Southern Brazil.
54. Eastern Brazil.

The above Maps are sold Separately. Each Map, Plain, 4d.; Coloured, 6d.

SHARPE—STUDENT'S ATLAS.

With a Copious Index. 26 Coloured Maps, selected from the preceding. Folio, half-bound. 21s.

SLACK—THE PHILOSOPHY OF PROGRESS IN

HUMAN AFFAIRS. By HENRY JAMES SLACK, F.G.S., Barrister-at-Law. Post 8vo., cloth. 6s.

SMITH (ALBERT)—WILD OATS AND DEAD LEAVES.

By ALBERT SMITH. Second Edition. Crown 8vo., cloth. 5s.

———— TO CHINA AND BACK:

BEING A DIARY KEPT OUT AND HOME. By ALBERT SMITH. 8vo. sewed. 1s.

SMITH (REV. JAMES)—THE DIVINE DRAMA OF
HISTORY AND CIVILIZATION. By the Rev. JAMES SMITH. 8vo. cloth. 12s.

——— (MRS.) — PRACTICAL AND ECONOMICAL
COOKERY, with a Series of Bills of Fare; also, Directions on Carving, Trussing, &c.
By MRS. SMITH, many years professed Cook to most of the leading families in the
Metropolis. Post 8vo. cloth. 5s. 6d.

STIGANT—A VISION OF BARBAROSSA, AND OTHER
POEMS. By WILLIAM STIGANT. Fcap. 8vo. cloth. 7s.

STORY (W. W.) — ROBA DI ROMA.
Second Edition. 2 vols. Post 8vo. cloth. 21s.

SYBEL (VON) — THE HISTORY AND LITERATURE
OF THE CRUSADES. By VON SYBEL. Translated by Lady DUFF GORDON. 1 vol.
post 8vo. 10s. 6d.

TANNHÄUSER, OR, THE BATTLE OF THE BARDS.
A Poem. By NEVILLE TEMPLE and EDWARD TREVOR. Fcap. 8vo. cloth. Fourth
Edition. 3s. 6d.

TAYLOR—PHILIP VAN ARTEVELDE. By HENRY
TAYLOR. Sixth edition. Fcap. 8vo. cloth. 3s. 6d.

——— EDWIN THE FAIR; ISAAC COMNENUS
THE EVE OF THE CONQUEST, AND OTHER POEMS. By HENRY TAYLOR.
Third edition. Fcap. 8vo. cloth. 3s. 6d.

——— ST. CLEMENT'S EVE: A DRAMA.
By HENRY TAYLOR, Author of 'Philip Van Artevelde,' &c. 1 vol. fcap. 5s.

THACKERAY—THE IRISH SKETCH-BOOK.
By M. A. TITMARSH. Fourth Edition, Uniform with Thackeray's 'Miscellaneous
Essays.' In crown 8vo. cloth, with Illustrations. 5s.

——— NOTES OF A JOURNEY FROM CORN-
HILL TO GRAND CAIRO, BY WAY OF LISBON, ATHENS, CONSTANTINOPLE,
AND JERUSALEM. By W. M. THACKERAY. With a Coloured Frontispiece.
Second Edition. Small 8vo. cloth. 6s.

——— CHRISTMAS BOOKS:
Containing 'MRS. PERKINS' BALL,' 'DR. BIRCH,' 'OUR STREET.' Cheap Edition.
In one square volume, cloth, with all the original Illustrations. 7s. 6d.

THURSTAN—THE PASSIONATE PILGRIM;
Or, EROS AND ANTEROS. By HENRY J. THURSTAN. Crown 8vo., cloth. 8s. 6d.

TILBURY NOGO;
Or, PASSAGES IN THE LIFE OF AN UNSUCCESSFUL MAN. By the Author of
'Digby Grand.' 2 vols. post 8vo. cloth. 21s. And New Edition, 1 vol. crown
8vo. 5s.

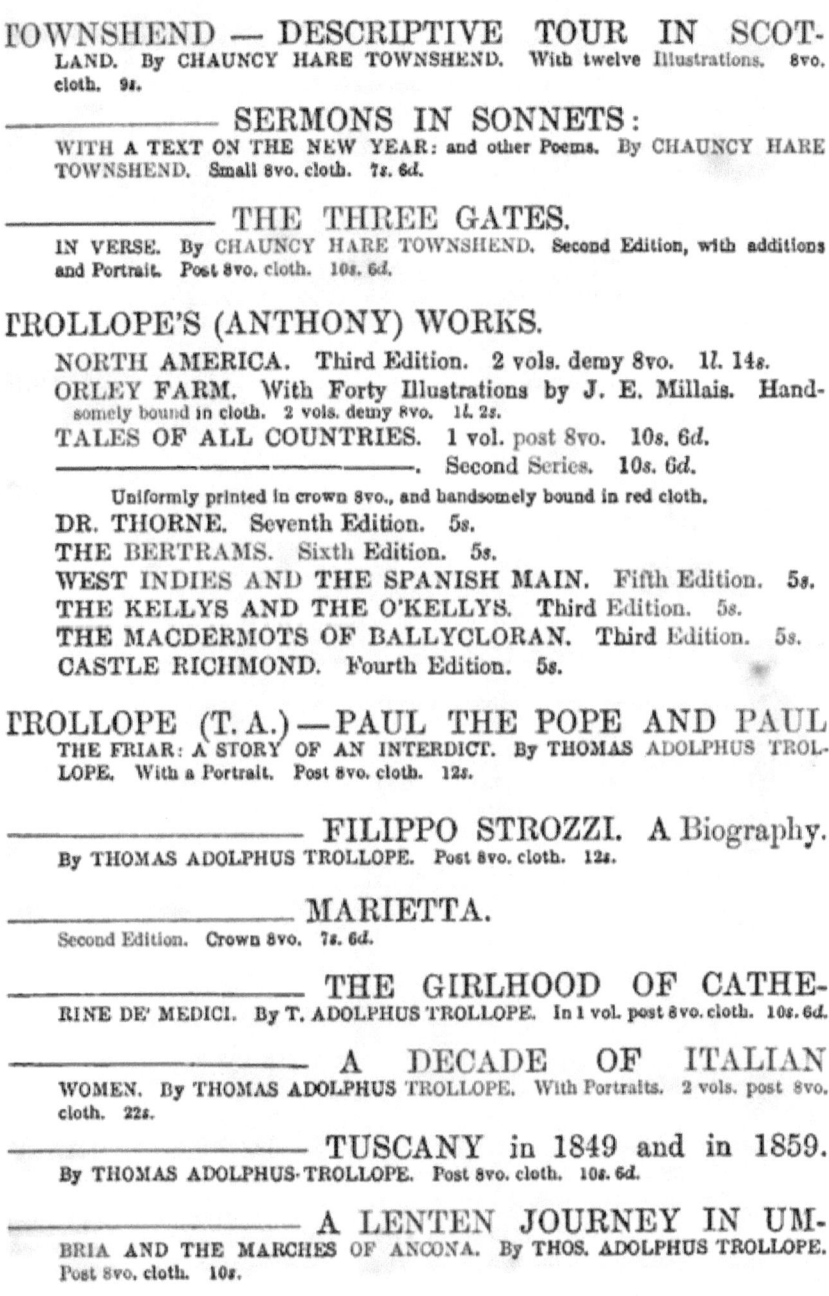

TOWNSHEND — DESCRIPTIVE TOUR IN SCOT-
LAND. By CHAUNCY HARE TOWNSHEND. With twelve Illustrations. 8vo.
cloth. 9s.

——————————— SERMONS IN SONNETS:
WITH A TEXT ON THE NEW YEAR: and other Poems. By CHAUNCY HARE
TOWNSHEND. Small 8vo. cloth. 7s. 6d.

——————————— THE THREE GATES.
IN VERSE. By CHAUNCY HARE TOWNSHEND. Second Edition, with additions
and Portrait. Post 8vo. cloth. 10s. 6d.

TROLLOPE'S (ANTHONY) WORKS.
NORTH AMERICA. Third Edition. 2 vols. demy 8vo. 1l. 14s.
ORLEY FARM. With Forty Illustrations by J. E. Millais. Hand-
somely bound in cloth. 2 vols. demy 8vo. 1l. 2s.
TALES OF ALL COUNTRIES. 1 vol. post 8vo. 10s. 6d.
—————————————————. Second Series. 10s. 6d.
Uniformly printed in crown 8vo., and handsomely bound in red cloth.
DR. THORNE. Seventh Edition. 5s.
THE BERTRAMS. Sixth Edition. 5s.
WEST INDIES AND THE SPANISH MAIN. Fifth Edition. 5s.
THE KELLYS AND THE O'KELLYS. Third Edition. 5s.
THE MACDERMOTS OF BALLYCLORAN. Third Edition. 5s.
CASTLE RICHMOND. Fourth Edition. 5s.

TROLLOPE (T. A.)—PAUL THE POPE AND PAUL
THE FRIAR: A STORY OF AN INTERDICT. By THOMAS ADOLPHUS TROL-
LOPE. With a Portrait. Post 8vo. cloth. 12s.

——————————— FILIPPO STROZZI. A Biography.
By THOMAS ADOLPHUS TROLLOPE. Post 8vo. cloth. 12s.

——————————— MARIETTA.
Second Edition. Crown 8vo. 7s. 6d.

——————————— THE GIRLHOOD OF CATHE-
RINE DE' MEDICI. By T. ADOLPHUS TROLLOPE. In 1 vol. post 8vo. cloth. 10s. 6d.

——————————— A DECADE OF ITALIAN
WOMEN. By THOMAS ADOLPHUS TROLLOPE. With Portraits. 2 vols. post 8vo.
cloth. 22s.

——————————— TUSCANY in 1849 and in 1859.
By THOMAS ADOLPHUS TROLLOPE. Post 8vo. cloth. 10s. 6d.

——————————— A LENTEN JOURNEY IN UM-
BRIA AND THE MARCHES OF ANCONA. By THOS. ADOLPHUS TROLLOPE.
Post 8vo. cloth. 10s.

TROLLOPE (THEODOSIA) — SOCIAL ASPECTS OI
REVOLUTION, IN A SERIES OF LETTERS FROM FLORENCE. Reprinted fron
the 'Athenæum.' With a Sketch of Subsequent Events up to the Present Time. B
THEODOSIA TROLLOPE. Post 8vo. cloth. 8s. 6d.

TWILIGHT THOUGHTS. By M. S. C.,
Author of ' Little Poems for Little People.' Second Edition, with a Frontispiece. Fca;
cloth. 1s. 6d.

TWINING — THE ELEMENTS OF PICTURESQUI
SCENERY; or, STUDIES OF NATURE MADE IN TRAVEL, with a View to In
provement in Landscape Painting. By HENRY TWINING. Vol. II. Imp. 8vo. cloth. 8

VANCE (ALEXANDER) — ROMANTIC EPISODE:
OF CHIVALRIC AMD MEDIÆVAL FRANCE; to which are appended some fe
Passages from Montaigne. Now done into English by ALEXANDER VANCE. Post 8v
cloth. 10s. 6d.

———————————————————————— THE HISTORY ANI
PLEASANT CHRONICLE OF LITTLE JEHAN DE SAINTE, AND OF THE LAD
OF THE FAIR COUSINS. Together with the Book of the Knight of the Tower, Landr
which he made for the Instruction of his Daughters. Now done into English by ALE?
ANDER VANCE. Post 8vo., cloth. 10s. 6d.

WAYFARING SKETCHES AMONG THE GREEK:
AND TURKS, AND ON THE SHORES OF THE DANUBE. By a Seven Yea:
Resident in Greece. Second Edition. Post 8vo. cloth. 9s.

WHIST-PLAYER (THE).
THE LAWS AND PRACTICE OF SHORT WHIST. EXPLAINED AND ILLUSTRATI
BY COLONEL BLYTH. With numerous Diagrams printed in Colours. Imp. 16m
Second Edition. 5s.

WHITE — A LONDONER'S WALK TO THE LAND'
END, AND A TRIP TO THE SCILLY ISLES. Second Edition. Post 8vo. clot
With four Maps. 4s.

———————— A MONTH IN YORKSHIRE.
By WALTER WHITE. Fourth Edition. With a Map. Post 8vo. cloth. 4s.

———————— ALL ROUND THE WREKIN.
By WALTER WHITE. Second Edition, post 8vo. cloth. 9s.

———————— NORTHUMBERLAND AND THE BORDEI
By WALTER WHITE. Second Edition. With a Map. Post 8vo. cloth. 10s. 6d.

———————— A JULY HOLIDAY IN SAXONY, BOHE
MIA AND SILESIA. By WALTER WHITE. Post 8vo. cloth. 9s.

WHITE—ON FOOT THROUGH TYROL ;
IN THE SUMMER OF 1855. By WALTER WHITE. Post 8vo. cloth. 9s.

WHITE—A SAILOR-BOY'S LOG-BOOK.
From Portsmouth to Peiho. With a Portrait. Edited by WALTER WHITE. 1 vol. crown 8vo. 5s.

WILKINSON (J. J. G.) — THE HUMAN BODY AND ITS
CONNEXION WITH MAN. Illustrated by the principal Organs. By JAMES JOHN GARTH WILKINSON. Post 8vo. cloth. 5s.

WILKINSON (W. M.) — THE REVIVAL IN ITS PHY-.
SICAL, PSYCHICAL, AND RELIGIOUS ASPECTS. By W. M. WILKINSON. Second Edition. Small 8vo. cloth. 3s. 6d.

WILLIAMS—HINTS ON THE CULTIVATION OF
BRITISH AND EXOTIC FERNS AND LYCOPODIUMS; with Descriptions of One Hundred and Fifty Species and Varieties. By BENJAMIN SAMUEL WILLIAMS. 8vo. cloth. 3s. 6d.

——————————— THE ORCHID-GROWER'S MANUAL ;
Containing a Brief Description of upwards of Two Hundred and Sixty Orchidaceous Plants, together with Notices of their times of Flowering, and most approved Modes of Treatment. By BENJAMIN SAMUEL WILLIAMS. With a Coloured Frontispiece. Second Edition. Post 8vo. cloth. 5s.

WILLS — OLD LEAVES GATHERED FROM 'HOUSE-
HOLD WORDS.' By W. HENRY WILLS. Post 8vo. cloth. 5s.

WORNUM — THE CHARACTERISTICS OF STYLES ;
An Introduction to the Study of the History of Ornamental Art. By RALPH N. WORNUM. In royal 8vo. cloth, with very many Illustrations. Second Edition. 8s.

WRIGHT — A HISTORY OF DOMESTIC MANNERS
AND SENTIMENTS IN ENGLAND DURING THE MIDDLE AGES. By THOMAS WRIGHT, M.A., F.S.A., Hon. M.R.S.L., &c.; Corresponding Member of the Imperial Institute of France (Académie des Inscriptions et Belles Lettres). Illustrated by upwards of 300 Engravings on Wood; with Illustrations from the Illuminations in Contemporary Manuscripts, and other sources, drawn and engraved by F. W. FAIRHOLT, F.S.A. In 1 vol. fcap. quarto, price 21s., bound in an appropriate ornamental cover.

YONGE — THE LIFE OF FIELD-MARSHAL ARTHUR,
DUKE OF WELLINGTON. By CHARLES DUKE YONGE. With Portrait, Plans, and Maps. 2 vols. 8vo. cloth. 40s.

——————— PARALLEL LIVES OF ANCIENT AND
MODERN HEROES, OF EPAMINONDAS, PHILIP OF MACEDON, GUSTAVUS ADOLPHUS, AND FREDERICK THE GREAT. By CHARLES DUKE YONGE, Author of 'A History of England,' &c. Small 8vo. cloth. 4s. 6d.

BOOKS FOR THE  USE OF SCHOOLS,

ISSUED UNDER THE

AUTHORITY OF THE

SCIENCE AND ART

DEPARTMENT,

SOUTH

KENSINGTON.

THE CHARACTERISTICS OF STYLES. An Introduction to the Study of the History of Ornamental Art. By RALPH N. WORNUM. Second Edition. In royal 8vo., with very many Illustrations. 8s.

BURCHETT'S LINEAR PERSPECTIVE. By R. BURCHETT, Fifth Edition. Post 8vo. With Illustrations. 7s.

BURCHETT'S DEFINITIONS OF GEOMETRY. 24mo. sewed. Third Edition. Price 5d.

BURCHETT'S PRACTICAL GEOMETRY. Fourth Edition. 8vo. cloth. Price 5s.

DYCE'S ELEMENTARY OUTLINES OF ORNAMENT. 50 Selected Plates, small folio, sewed. Price 5s.

TEXT TO DYCE'S DRAWING ROOM. Fcap. 8vo. Price 6d.

REDGRAVE'S MANUAL AND CATECHISM ON COLOUR. Second Edition. 24mo. sewed. Price 9d.

REDGRAVE ON THE NECESSITY OF PRINCIPLES IN TEACHING DESIGN. Fcap. sewed. Price 6d.

A DIAGRAM TO ILLUSTRATE THE HARMONIOUS RE-LATIONS OF COLOUR. Small folio. Price 9d.

PRINCIPLES OF DECORATIVE ART. Folio. sewed. Price 1s.

LINDLEY'S SYMMETRY OF VEGETATION. 8vo. sewed. Price 1s.

ROBINSON'S LECTURES ON THE MUSEUM. Fcap. sewed. Price 6d.

AN ALPHABET OF COLOUR. Reduced from the works of Field, Hay, Chevreuil. 4to. sewed. Price 3s.

DIRECTIONS FOR INTRODUCING ELEMENTARY DRAWING IN SCHOOLS AND AMONG WORKMEN. Published at the request of the Society of Arts. Small 4to. cloth. Price 4s. 6d.

ILLUSTRATIONS TO BE EMPLOYED IN THE PRAC-TICAL LESSONS ON BOTANY. Adapted to all classes. Prepared for the South Kensington Museum. By the REV. PROF. HENSLOW. With Illustrations. Post 8vo. Price 6d.

DRAWING FOR ELEMENTARY SCHOOLS: Being a Manual of the Method of Teaching Drawing, specially adapted for the Use of Masters of National and Parochial Schools. By ELLIS A. DAVIDSON, Head Master of the Chester School of Art. Published under the sanction of the Science and Art Department of the Committee of Council of Education. Post 8vo. cloth. 3s.

ELEMENTS OF GEOMETRICAL DRAWING; or Practical Geometry, Plane and Solid, including both Orthographic and Perspective Projection. Illustrated by Sixty Plates, engraved by J. W. Lowry, from original drawings. By THOMAS BRADLEY, of the Royal Military Academy, Woolwich, and Professor of Geometrical Drawing at King's College, London. Published for the Committee of Council on Education. In Two Parts, oblong folio, cloth, 16s. each.

LONDON : PRINTED BY W. CLOWES AND SONS, STAMFORD STREET, AND CHARING CROSS.

www.ingramcontent.com/pod-product-compliance
Lightning Source LLC
Chambersburg PA
CBHW031346070726
47496CB00017B/1798